A HAND TO EXECUTE

A HAND TO EXECUTE

Randy Lee Eickhoff

Walker and Company
New York

First published in the United States of America in 1987 by the Walker Publishing Company, Inc.

Published simultaneously in Canada by John Wiley & Sons Canada, Limited, Rexdale, Ontario.

Library of Congress Cataloging-in-Publication Data

Eickhoff, Randy Lee
    A hand to execute.

    "A Walker adventure novel."
PS3555.I23H3   1987   813'.54   86-32527
ISBN 0-8027-0964-8

Printed in the United States of America

10 9 8 7 6 5 4 3 2 1

To Dianne,
my wife, my friend,
my lover,
and to my children,
Randy Roger and Leone

Acknowledgments

A FIRST NOVELIST owes a great debt to so many people that it is almost impossible to remember them all. Those who come immediately to mind are Cleo Martin at the University of Iowa whose friendship and faith in my writing kept me at the typewriter; Vance Bourjaily, who convinced me to polish, polish, polish; my editor Philip Turner, who was willing to take a gamble; Jim Pearson, who continually reminded me I was a writer; W. Earl Dyer, Jr. and Hal Brown (RIP), who taught me some fine points invaluable for a young writer who thinks he knows everything; Don Walton, who taught me to look beneath what people were saying; and many, many others. Others have dimmed with memory, others cannot be named such as those who walked the streets of Saigon with me in 1965 and the mountains of Vietnam in 1966. Some of these names one can find on the Vietnam War Memorial which is far more fitting than mention here.

"Whether it be the heart to conceive, the understanding to direct, or the hand to execute."

Junius: *Letter 37*
(19 March 1770)

Author's Note

MOST OF THE characters in this work are the result of the author's imagination and if some enterprising soul thinks he may have found a case for a *roman à clef,* I suggest he examine the work from a broader perspective. What follows is fiction although there is, as in all fiction, a touch of truth present. I leave it up to the reader to discover the truth and, in the process, enjoy the fiction.

A HAND TO EXECUTE

1

THE TELEGRAM WAS waiting for me at the bar of the Continental when I returned from the Special Forces camp at Plei Me. I sighed, slipped my thumb under the seal, and opened it. It was from the American Embassy, informing me that my assistant had been killed in a skirmish at the Michelin Plantation. No "we regrets" and no information on what had been done with the body, just twelve succinct words from someone named MOORE. I reread it, laid it on the table in front of me, and picked up the first gin and tonic of the day, sipping it.

I had no idea why Jerry Muhl had gone to the Michelin Plantation. When I left Saigon on the press plane for Nha Trang, he was on his way to the United States Information Service (USIS) auditorium for the daily press conference. Ordinarily, our roles would have been reversed, and he would have gone to Nha Trang while I attended the press conference, but I had met a friend at the Mekong Floating Restaurant the night before who claimed the information we had been receiving concerning the North Vietnamese People's Army (NVA) buildup around Plei Me was less than accurate. He suggested it might be worth my while if I made a little trip to Nha Trang. I could hitch a ride on one of the helicopters resupplying the Special Forces base camps outside of Plei Me and see for myself. I followed his advice, sent Muhl to the daily conference, and made the trip to Plei Me. My source was right: there was a massive buildup of Vietminh regulars around the Special Forces camp, and the casualty figures much different according to front line officers than those supplied to us by the Military Assistance Command-Vietnam (MAC-V).

My first story from Plei Me was also my last. I was quickly bundled onto a C-130 cargo plane returning to Ton Son Nuht and given a subtle warning not to visit any troops without first requesting permission through MAC-V. It was my third such warning and tempers were beginning to fray. But that was no problem: the warnings were standard issue to newsmen, like GI underwear to the troops.

As I sat and watched the traffic in Lam Lon Square, I tried to think of a reason for Muhl to have skipped the conference and gone to the plantation. There had been no news at the Michelin Plantation for over a year, although rumors of heavy Vietcong recruitment in that area had been trickling down to the press corps for the past few months. Still, I doubted if that was the reason for the change in plans. All the pressure seemed to be coming at Plei Me in the north and the Delta in the south. A few bands of guerrillas were concentrated in what MAC-V liked to call "the safe areas," but they really accounted for very little and were largely ignored by those of us who had been in the country for any length of time. These small bands were usually reserved for the newcomer who needed a few quick stories to convince his editor he was the next Hemingway. Muhl was green, but not that green.

"Bad news does travel quickly, doesn't it?"

I looked up at the white-suited figure of Dupree. He pointed a planter's hat with a garish brown paisley band at the telegram on the table.

"What else could it be?" I said. "No good news ever comes by telegram these days. Will you have a drink?"

"Thank you." He pulled a chair away from the table and sat down. Carefully, he laid his hat on the chair next to him. Dupree was an enigma; no one knew precisely

2

what he did. He seemed to be on the periphery of the embassy crowd, but he did not have an office at the embassy and was never seen around "Lincoln Library," as the CIA boys were fond of calling their building on Le Qui Don Street. Actually, Lincoln Library was headquarters for the USIS, but that was an old joke among the veteran press, who privately held their suspicions to themselves.

"I'm terribly sorry," he began.

"He knew what he was doing," I said.

"And what was that?"

"Ah. Freedom of the press, you know."

"Perhaps in your country," he said, smiling thinly, "but I'm afraid we still have censorship here. A mild form, anyway."

"You're beginning to sound like a policeman," I said. "Are you a policeman?"

"No. I am a broker. Surely you knew that?" He signaled to a waiter, pointed at my glass, and raised two fingers. His manicured nails flashed briefly in the sunlight.

"How long had he been over here?"

I ignored him. Why should I tell him how long Muhl had been here? The answer was perfectly obvious: long enough to get himself killed. Six months, to be precise. He had walked across the square directly to this table, where I had been sitting with the second or third gin and tonic of the day and a pile of notes from Westmoreland's latest conference. I was trying to work the notes into a new angle for the *Times*. He was fresh and eager, the stateside haircut still seen in the white around his ears. He seemed all arms and legs, and his freckled face was wreathed in a smile as, without waiting for an invitation, he pulled a chair out and sat down.

"Hi," he said. "My name's Muhl. Like in Missouri, but not so stubborn. I'm your new legs." He looked at

3

me expectantly. I must have been frowning, for the smile slipped a little from his face.

"You *are* Connie Edwards?"

"Con," I corrected. "At least, that's what it says on the byline."

"Oh-oh. I think I touched a nerve."

He had. I have never liked being called "Connie." It was much too familiar and sounded like dark nights in the back seat of a DeSoto.

He turned to watch the young ladies walk by in their white *ao dais,* ankle-length white silk trousers with tunics slit to the thigh. A man never tired of seeing them and would never forget them as they flitted like butterflies about the square, for they would remind him every day of his youth.

"I think I'm going to like it here," he said. "Lots of lovelies."

I flinched. He had an extraordinary way of destroying the innocence of dreams. A useful tool for a reporter, but a hindrance for a newsman who occasionally had to deal with dreams. But that was something not taught in the best journalism schools in the States. I knew he came from one of the best, for the *Times* had moved with the future and no longer promoted copy boys to reporters and reporters to editors. His arrival in Saigon was a sign of what was to come. Old newsmen like me would no longer be promoted to editorships; those positions would be saved for the Muhls. We would simply be their trainers. I had long accepted this as the reason I had not been recalled from Indochina. I was the oldest newsman still on a beat, but to recall me would mean promotion, and that type of promotion was, in the parlance of the trade, a "closed shop." I had accepted this, but I didn't like it.

"Well," he said and turned back to me, the grin still easy on his lips. "What's the first order of business?"

4

"I suggest an introduction," I said a little stiffly.

"Do you mind?" he asked and reached for my gin and tonic. "It's terribly hot." He drank half the glass and replaced it.

"Help yourself," I said sarcastically and motioned for the boy to bring another. "But wouldn't it be easier just to order one for yourself?"

"Huh?" He had turned back to the square. I had a funny feeling he didn't understand. The young are like that these days. They slip in and out of conversation like fog.

"Would you care for a drink?" I patiently asked.

"If you like," he said and shrugged his shoulders indifferently. "But I don't want to overdo it."

Was there a suggestion behind those words? A hint that I had been drinking too much? I seethed, but held my temper.

"Introduction?" I asked.

"Sorry?" He looked at me blankly.

"Who *are* you?"

"I'm your legs."

"You said that, but the last time I looked they were still attached to my torso and had not given birth."

"Oh. I'm sorry." He looked appalled. "Didn't you get the cablegram?"

"No."

"Oh." I was beginning to wonder if that word was a tenth of his vocabulary.

"I'm Jerry Muhl. The *Times* sent me to be your new assistant."

My new assistant? Why? Had I not been handling the bureau successfully for the past sixteen years by myself? What did I need an assistant for? The press conference was held daily at ten forty-five and lasted until noon. From noon until three I handled what human interest stories might suggest themselves, filed my copy by five,

5

and that pretty much took care of the Vietnam war coverage as provided by the *Times* man on the scene. What need was there for a larger bureau? Unless I was about to be shelved. My God! Was *this* to be my replacement?

"Are you writing a book?" I asked Dupree. I softened my words to make them unoffensive and was rewarded with another tight smile, his teeth even and white in the tan of his face.

"God help us," he said. "I'm afraid that would be more your line. I do not handle the language well enough for that. Besides, who would be interested in a book by a small broker?"

"Who indeed?" I murmured and sipped from my glass.

"Why was he at the Michelin Plantation?"

"I don't know."

His eyebrows raised fractionally. I could see he did not believe me.

"I thought you were senior in your bureau?"

"I was. Am. But I was at Plei Me. He was supposed to be at the press conference. I do not know why he decided to go to the plantation. Are you sure you are not a policeman?"

He ignored my chiding. "Why did you go to Plei Me?"

"To see my mistress."

"Comment?"

"You're a Frenchman. Surely you can understand these things."

"Affairs of the heart? Of course. Except you have no mistress in Plei Me."

"How do you know?"

"Because you have a mistress on the Rue Richard." Like all Frenchmen, he persisted in the old names. The Rue Richard had become Phan Dinh Phung after the French were defeated at Dien Bien Phu.

6

"And she is an American. Rather unusual for here. Most Americans would have taken Annamites. Do you not care for the local, ah, product?"

I wondered if he had been a member of the *Sûreté*. Perhaps he had and after the French defeat could have linked himself to the Hoa Haos or the Caodists or General The. He might even have been associated with the Binh Xuyen that controlled crime in Saigon the way the Mafia did in Chicago during the twenties. Supposedly, the private army of the Binh Xuyen had been disbanded by Diem's troops in '65, but one knew inexplicably that crime is never wiped out; it becomes more subtle.

"Did not Muhl once try to, how shall I put it, take her away from you?"

"I don't believe that is any of your affair," I said coldly. The answer, of course, was yes, as many knew. Muhl had taken advantage of my absence when I went to Hue two months after his arrival. I was digging up a story concerning some army first sergeants who had opened a string of whorehouses, stocking them with refugees from relocation camps under their command. It was a sordid story of the type that would not do U.S.-Vietnamese relations any good. Consequently, the army tried to bury it. My resurrection of the story led to a congressional investigation and did little to cement my relations with the army brass. The young soldiers not involved with army politics loved it, so little harm was done to my inside sources. Most of my tips came from them anyway.

When I returned, Ed Logan, UPI writer and friend, told me about Muhl's repeated visits to my apartment during my absence.

"Maybe he was just being friendly," I replied. "After all, there's not much for him to do when I'm gone."

"She went with him to the Cercle Sportif a couple of times," Logan said. "There's been talk."

"What kind of talk?"

"Cuckold talk," he said. He looked uncomfortable and avoided my eyes.

"It's rather common knowledge," Dupree said. "You made sure of that. I hope you're not offended?"

"Why should I be offended?" I asked. I was, though. The incident had been unpleasant. Rachel had denied doing anything other than dining with Muhl, and I believed her. I should have let it drop there, but I didn't, and the next day at lunch, I warned Muhl to keep away from her.

"Don't worry," he said. "I won't trespass in your territory. The war has left plenty of natives to choose from, and there is less chance of permanence with them."

"I don't think I care for your attitude," I said.

"Sorry. No offense."

"There's no reason to be so cavalier," I said. "You need to learn the difference between a *putain* and a *demoiselle*. There are many who will take exception to your actions."

"You are beginning to sound very colonial," he said, smiling easily, and leaned back carefully in his chair. "Aren't you forgetting that we are in a war zone?"

"What's that supposed to mean?"

"I think you know the proverb about love and war?" His eyes crinkled with amusement.

"I believe," I said slowly, trying to control my anger, "I believe you had better apologize."

"You're making a damn fool of yourself," he said softly. "Look around."

I glanced at the other tables and realized my anger had made my voice climb. The diners at the tables nearest us were pointedly involved with their meals.

"It would be even more foolish for you to become physical," he continued. "I have at least fifteen years on you and twenty pounds."

8

* * *

He was right; I had been very foolish. But even recognizing my foolishness did not make me any the less angry. The opposite was true; I seethed even more when he confronted me with my own helplessness. Muhl was like that. He seemed to enjoy playing games with other men's weaknesses.

"I am glad," Dupree said. "One should not offend one's friends. One always has enough enemies, but never enough friends."

"True," I said. I reached for the gin and tonic and sipped at it.

"Was Muhl a friend of yours?"

"Muhl was an ambitious man."

"And . . . ," he prompted.

"Ambitious men cannot afford friends."

"Aren't you being rather hard on him?"

"No," I replied. "He was hard on himself. He had many goals he set for himself and not enough time to involve himself in doing the groundwork to reach those goals. He was very impatient."

"Not a very good epitaph," Dupree speculated.

"No."

"And yet, he seemed to be very successful. I read some of his work. It was quite good."

"In some things," I relented. "But he was beginning to lose his perspective. He was getting too involved. War was becoming virtuous for him."

Dupree toyed with his drink, making a series of connected circles on the table with the condensation on the bottom of the glass. Abruptly, I noticed that the glass was still almost full, and I wondered again if Dupree was a policeman. And what if he was a policeman? What did that mean to me? I had been somewhere near Nha Trang when Muhl was killed.

"It is too bad you do not know what he was doing at the Michelin Plantation," he said quietly. His eyes flickered to mine, then back to the table, but not before I caught the guarded interest in them. I decided to ignore his suggestion.

"Do you know where the body is?"

"The police have it," he said. He flicked his fingers at a fly that buzzed inquisitively around the rim of his glass.

"The police?" I was surprised.

"Yes."

"There is some question about his death?"

"There is always a question about a death," he said. With a sudden fluid movement, he raised the glass to his lips and drained its contents. He rose, picked up his hat, and settled it carefully on his head.

"You will have to identify him, I believe," he said.

"Why?" I asked.

"Its a routine," he said soothingly. "Unpleasant, I know, but it has to be done. Since he was a civilian, the military authorities cannot help. The police have the only other deepfreeze in Saigon."

"I see." I finished my drink and motioned to the waiter for a refill. "And when do you think I should do this?"

"The sooner, the better," he said apologetically and spread his hands. "The climate, you know."

"Tell me, Dupree," I said. "Tell me. The truth, now. Are you a policeman?"

He laughed politely, touched the brim of his hat, and left. I watched him as he moved elegantly across the square. A trishaw driver slowed by him, but he waved the driver away. I remembered his questions and smiled; he was as much a policeman as I was a reporter. But for whom? That reminded me. I turned and called to the waiter to bring me a cable pad. I had an obituary to write. I wondered how drunk I needed to get before writing it. Vitriolic prose does not make an acceptable obituary, and I had some lying to do.

10

2

BY THE TIME I had finished with Muhl's obituary and filed it at the cable office, I decided I was drunk enough to make the visit to police headquarters. I called a trishaw and directed the driver to take me to the old *Sûreté* building. I pretended not to notice the uneasiness in his eyes. The police force in Saigon these days was highly unpredictable. Total strangers had been snatched off the street, accused of being Vietcong sympathizers, and sent to prison camps after only a few displaced bones, if they were lucky. If not, they were shot. Or perhaps they were lucky to be shot. I had heard stories about those camps, uneasy stories that made Treblinka sound like a ballet.

The trishaw driver did not linger at police headquarters looking for a return fare. He took the money from my outstretched hand and immediately turned back for Tu Do Street, his thickly muscled legs pumping furiously. I didn't blame him. The building was an odious gray and smelled of urine and death. Four Vietnamese guards lounged lazily next to the door and insolently watched me as I passed them and entered the building.

The receptionist was looking through a book of pornographic pictures. I recognized it as one of the more recent arrivals at the bookstalls near the Quay Gremaine de Pres and wondered who had been put out of business. I hoped whoever it was had friends with the Binh Xuyen and those friends would know which officials could be bribed. Otherwise, I knew it would be a long time before he saw the quay again.

I explained my presence to the receptionist and waited patiently while he sent for someone to take me to the morgue. It was a mark of Vietnamese efficiency that the messenger stationed at the receptionist's desk could not himself guide me to the morgue. Instead, he would return with another messenger who would lead me to a minor official who would then dispatch that messenger to another office higher up in the hierarchy who would repeat the performance until one finally led me to the morgue. In the meantime, I would waste an hour doing a fifteen-minute job while several minor officials demonstrated the need for their offices.

After two trips up and down the stained marble steps, I ended in a cramped office only four doors from where I had waited for the first messenger. I was rather surprised to discover it was the office of Le Duc Trinh, the top assistant to Nguyen Ngoc Loan, the fanatical chief of police who ruthlessly searched out Vietcong agents within the city. I sighed. The simple identification procedure seemed to have magnified into something a bit more ominous. Le Duc Trinh did not involve himself in anything as minor as a dead Western correspondent unless state security was in the picture somewhere. A few years back he had cleverly built a case against the Buddhists that allowed Ky's predecessor, Diem, to move into the temples and eliminate the dissidents who were trying to disrupt the September elections by making them fair. Although he kept himself discreetly out of the bloodletting that followed when Diem turned his troops loose, we all knew who had been the catalyst for Diem's actions.

He looked like an ascetic lizard as he sat behind his desk, thumbing through a heavy file while he studiously ignored me. The smell of opium was heavy in the room, and I wondered how long it had been since his last pipe.

Opium often made the user dogmatic and senseless to reason, and I had no desire to have my press credentials revoked and my exit visa held up in red tape. Nor did I really want to spend a vacation on the prison island of Poulo Condore south of Vietnam, where many had mysteriously disappeared. I knew a correspondent who had suddenly lost his translator. He had traced him to this building, and, after running into several stone walls with his questions, he had threatened the officers with official investigation from the government. He had been taken to a small office such as this, shown a few photographs of Poulo Condore, and was given a polite suggestion to let the issue drop. He did and never saw his translator again.

At last, Le Duc Trinh looked up and his death's-head smile gleamed in the darkness at me.

"Ah. Mr. Edwards. How nice of you to come." He spoke softly and elegantly, his syntax betraying his Cambridge education, but the words were marred by the sibilance of his speech, a reptilian impediment that changed the amenity to a threat.

"Anything to help," I murmured. I tried to sound casual, noncommittal.

"The willingness of those who enter this room to cooperate always amazes me," he said. "I have found that their willingness is compounded by their feelings of guilt."

"One way or another, I suppose?"

"Shall we say that at times memories have to be refreshed?"

"Or informed?" I ventured gently.

He frowned, and I mentally rebuked myself for the gin and tonic carelessness.

"You understand the difficulties that sometimes arise with exit visas?" The sibilance was more pronounced, and I knew I had irritated him.

"I presume I'll not be needing one for a while," I said.

13

"At least, my editors have not notified me of any changes they might be considering," I added as a precaution that he did not misinterpret the intent of my words.

"Then," he smiled and thrust his head forward, "then since you are staying, perhaps we should be friends."

"That would be nice," I managed. Friendship with Le Duc Trinh would dry up most of my sources among the Vietnamese. A cobra and his Indian fakir may get along famously together, but I would wager a year's salary against a fistful of sous that the fakir doesn't get invited many places for dinner.

"Yes," he said and leaned back in his chair. He drummed his fingers on the file in front of him and looked past me to the door. His eyes became distant as his thoughts turned inward. I was reminded again of the ascetic lizard.

"Now that we are friends, perhaps you can tell me why your associate went to the Michelin Plantation." His voice was again soft, the sibilant hardly noticeable.

"Sorry. I don't know." He frowned, and I hastened to explain. "I was in Nha Trang. He was supposed to cover the daily conference. I did not know about any change of plans or even that he had been killed until I returned."

"Actually," he murmured, "you were in Plei Me. But I understand your reluctance. Newsmen always respect their sources. Are you suggesting he acted on his own initiative?"

"Looks that way."

"Are you the senior man in your office?"

"Yes. Was and still am."

"And yet, you claim he did not inform you of his intentions?"

"I don't claim anything. I'm just telling you the situation."

"Of course you are," he said smoothly. "Why would you not?"

I didn't answer him. The question did not need an answer, the implication was there. Like Dupree, Trinh was a master of insinuation. If I had any feeling for Muhl at all, it had thoroughly dissipated. I resented his death, I resented his impulsive decision to go to the Michelin Plantation, and I resented him for getting himself killed and forcing me to be here, now, in this room in front of this man.

"Was he political?" Trinh asked.

"My God," I answered. "He was a reporter. Though not a very good one," I added.

"You have not answered my question."

"I don't know. I suppose as far as any of us are political he was political."

"But he never voiced any views to you?"

"No."

"I don't believe you."

I wasn't surprised. I wouldn't have believed it either. But I had no intention of sitting in that dark office for the rest of the day trying to explain how journalists work to a mind looking only for guilt. The least nuance or offhand remark could be twisted onto a path of questioning until even the most seasoned journalist lost track of the initial question, and right now, given the gin and tonics I had consumed, I was the most "seasoned" journalist in Vietnam. Consequently, I simply shrugged and tried to look like I wasn't hiding anything.

"You are a fool, Mr. Edwards. Either a fool or a very clever man," he said softly. His eyes told me nothing; he could have been calculating whether I was worth sending to Poulo Condore or if I was simply stupid. I turned my attention to the framed photographs on his desk. A plump, middle-aged woman, one step away from homeliness, smiled prettily from one photo while two children, a boy and girl dressed in a military uniform and *ao dai*, respectively, looked at the camera impassively, as children have always looked at cameras. I tried to picture Trinh as a family man, but couldn't. He belonged to whips and chains, branding irons and bamboo splinters, rather than Sundays in the park and loving arms in the dark.

"Your job predicates cooperation," he said. "Without cooperation, where would you be?"

"Home?" I suggested.

He smiled. "And doing what? Writing that famous novel all newsmen claim to have within them? Or your famous exploits in the exotic Far East? Do you fancy yourself another Maugham, Mr. Edwards?"

He was right. What was there for me back home? More rejection slips from apologetic publishers? "We regret this doesn't quite measure up to our standards, etc." Trinh was right. I needed situations like this, and I needed the cooperation of the officials. A closed door would severely limit my coverage.

"What do you want?" I asked. "I really don't know that much about him. We had nothing in common."

"Your work," he murmured. He lifted a small silver letter opener from his desk and began toying with it.

"Not even that," I said. "He really wasn't that good. I had to edit most of his work before placing it on the wire."

"A very superior attitude," he said.

"Not at all. You asked, I told you. He was really more a liability than help."

"Then he was not your friend?"

How to answer that? There were times when he could be very charming and pleasant to be with, and he wasn't hesitant when it came time to pick up the check. Perhaps if it had not been for his interest in Rachel I would have been more receptive towards him. But Rachel had been living with me for two years before Muhl was assigned to my bureau. We were lovers, but really weren't in love.

16

We were fond and comfortable with each other and through that fondness became each other's haven. Muhl did not cause any friction between us, at first, but his intrusion into our lives threatened the harmony that had grown between us. He seemed to take a perverse pleasure in making us feel uncomfortable.

One evening while Rachel and I were dining at the Continental, we were rudely joined by Muhl, who pulled a chair away from a neighboring table and sat without invitation. I was further piqued when he slid the chair as close as possible to Rachel.

"Slumming?" he asked. He'd had a few drinks (I could smell the Scotch on his breath) and tried to look down Rachel's blouse, but she picked up her wine glass and leaned back in her chair away from him. He laughed and picked up my wine glass and tasted it.

"Mm. Good. Lafitte. A provincial wine."

"Rothschild," I corrected and signaled to the waiter to bring a clean glass.

"I should've known," he said. "You always go for labels, don't you?"

I ignored the jibe and lifted the bottle from the silver bucket and offered it to him.

"Would you like some more?"

"No." He placed the glass upside down on the snowy white linen. A ruby red bead ran down the side of the glass and soaked into the tablecloth.

"I would prefer something with more body." He leered at Rachel. "Something like you."

"Now just a minute . . . ," I began hotly.

"It's all right, Con," Rachel said. She stared at him coldly. "I like labels, too. Would you care to hear which I have in mind for you?"

"Ah, ah." He wagged his finger at her in mock derision. "That's a modern woman talking. You can't be a modern woman and have ol' provincial Con here. Now I, on the other hand, like modern women."

"Why don't you leave?" I bluntly suggested.

"Why do you come here?" he asked. "Everyone else goes to the Caravelle."

"That's why I come here," I said. "I like the atmosphere."

"A bit seedy now," he commented, while looking around him. "In the old days you couldn't have afforded it."

"In the old days you wouldn't have been allowed in the front door, much less to the terrace," I said.

"You know what your problem is?" He seemed to be getting annoyed.

"No, but I'm sure you're going to tell me," I said. I picked up the wine bottle and held it idly in my hand even though my glass was still half-full.

"You're an antediluvian," he said with satisfaction. "Everything about you is outdated, from your convoluted prose to your old-fashioned principles of gentlemanly honor and fair play. You seem to find something picturesque, almost quixotic, about this splendid little war, despite the deaths and tortures the rest of us see. No, Con, you are not very hard to understand, and that's the pity of it all, for you don't understand. You've been out here too long. You've lost your perspective."

I replaced the bottle of wine in its bucket and carefully pressed my hands flat on the table to hide their trembling. I tried to tell myself that he was drunk and mad at the way I had rewritten his piece on the growing numbers in the relocation camps. Muhl had not approached the article from the viewpoint of cultural shock (which was suggested by the indiscriminate mixing of tribes and beliefs under the bureaucratic assumption that the Vietnamese were either hostiles or friendlies) and the relocation economics. He had tried to write an inflammatory

18

exposé on the living conditions of the refugees in the camps without documentary sources or even soliciting an official reply. Instead of remaining clinical and passive, he had forgotten, in his zeal, the first dictum of a reporter: Do not get involved. Rather than censure him for this, I had simply reduced his story to the five hundred words the situation demanded and forwarded the article to the *Times* along with a memo that we would plan an in-depth follow-up in case the situation warranted. I tried to tell myself that his bad manners were caused by this, but the smirk on his face made me unreasonable.

"The barren writing you have a tendency to submit as finished pieces forces me to have little regard for your literary judgment. You have little background for making the assumptions you claim as fact. You do not know anything about the feudal society that Saigon was once and, to a certain extent, still is, nor do you understand the peasant mind. It takes a lifetime to understand these things and not a few weeks spent in crash courses studying isms and theories in passionless textbooks."

My voice shook from the intensity of my words, and Rachel leaned across the table and pressed my hand. Muhl smiled sardonically and mockingly clapped his hands.

"Bravo," he said. "Now why don't you write like that?"

"Get out," I said thickly. "Get out, or I'll call the waiter."

"I'll leave," he said and rose insolently to his feet. "But if you think about it, you'll see I'm right. You need more compassion and passion in your writing instead of the soft pap you've been peddling."

After he left we tried to regain the gaiety of the moment, but too much tension remained at the table for comfort and tranquility. Even the wine seemed to have turned from his presence. But I knew, after a fashion, he was correct: my work had become dry and arid, and what I called conciseness was really melancholic writing, staid and stuffy. I was no longer absorbed in the dilemmas of war and had stopped looking for the truth. I had become a chronicler of facts and figures, a statistical role player who ignored the humanity behind the columns of the dead and missing-in-action.

"I asked if he was your friend."

I blinked and pulled my thoughts back to the dark office and Trinh.

"He caused a lot of trouble," I said tentatively. "He was very rash and often became too close to his subjects."

"Yes," said Trinh. "We are not sorry that he is dead."

His eyes never left my face. Did he expect me to react with indignation at his callousness? If so, he was disappointed, for I had drunk too many gin and tonics and was too tired from the Plei Me flight to take offense. Outrage was burned from me, and all I wanted was to take a look at the body, agree that it was Muhl, arrange to have his effects sent home, and take myself home to Rachel.

"There is nothing you wish to tell me?" Trinh asked. His eyes glittered malevolently over the desk towards me. What, I wondered, did he want me to tell him? He knew everything about Muhl that I did and probably more. I told him so.

"Not even about Molly?"

"Who?"

"Molly. Was she a friend or," he searched for the appropriate word, "paramour of your associate?"

"I don't know anyone by that name. Molly? No."

"You are sure?"

"Yes. I would tell you if I knew because there would be no reason not to. I've told you everything I can."

20

"You've told me nothing," he said and slid his chair away from his desk. He stood and silently looked at me. For the first time I noticed how slight he was, thin, almost skeletal, a personification of death, the leading role in Poe's "Masque."

"Come with me," he said abruptly and led the way out of his office. We crossed the hall to a small, cramped stairwell that smelled strongly of urine and vomit and walked four flights down to the subterranean morgue. The light was dim, but the porcelain of the drawers gleamed whitely like bones. A taciturn attendant in a soiled white jacket led us to one of the drawers and pulled it open. The refrigeration unit began to hum noisily and I found myself looking at Muhl. His lips were pulled back in a wolfish grin, and his eyes were half-lidded. He had an ugly bruise high on the left side of his forehead, and a dried streak of blood ran from his left ear down his cheek to the hollow of his throat.

"Well?" Trinh asked.

"Yes," I said. For some reason I had to tell myself I was innocent and did not belong there smelling the decay and choking back the harsh tonic that threatened to burst from my mouth.

"I thought he was shot."

"He was." Trinh pulled back the sheet and pointed at Muhl's chest. I was surprised by the absence of blood. There was just a small, blue-gray hole stark against the pallid skin just above the left nipple.

I turned to go and bumped the drawer with my hip. Muhl's arm fell from beneath the sheet. The fingernails on his right hand were missing. I swallowed rapidly and looked away.

"I think," I said slowly, "the question is where he was shot."

"That has been answered," Trinh said. He casually slipped Muhl's arm back under the sheet.

"No. You do not understand. I mean site."

"The Michelin Plantation," Trinh said. His eyes burrowed into mine. "He was shot at the Michelin Plantation. But what he was doing there, we do not know."

Sharply, he ordered the attendant to close the drawer, and Muhl slid once again into darkness. The drawer sealed itself as the refrigeration unit pumped out cold air.

"Can I pick up his things?" I asked as we climbed the steps back to his office.

"In a few days," Trinh said. "When we are through with them."

"And the body?"

"Ah, yes. That may take some time," he said, a hint of apology to his words. Or, was it sarcasm?

I stopped on the landing and looked down at him. "Why? What is the problem?"

"The problem," he said smoothly, "is the paperwork. You must sign a statement of release, another to claim the body, then produce transit papers for the shipment of the body to your country. In addition, the papers must be filed with the Bureau of Statistics and countersigned by an official of that department. Then we can release the body."

I stared at him in disbelief. The Bureau of Statistics was a maze of red tape impossible to find one's way through. I had tried to trace a Vietnamese friend of mine who had disappeared at the outbreak of the revolt against Diem and had given up in despair after three weeks of shuttling from one office to another and back. Besides, this couldn't be the procedure for all the American dead daily shipped back home. The paperwork would be a Matterhorn of transfer impossible to move.

"Muhl was not an official or a soldier," Trinh explained after I voiced my misgivings.

"Then what was he?"

"A civilian." He walked into his office and closed the

22

door behind him. I stared at the peeling paint for a moment, then left.

Out in the bright sunlight I breathed deeply, trying to erase the smell of the building. But the city itself seemed impregnated with the stench, and all I accomplished was to make myself dizzy from hyperventilating. I looked for a taxi or trishaw, but the streets were clear and I sighed and trudged back towards Le Loi Boulevard. I did not know what Le Duc Trinh was looking for, and I did not care for Muhl's sake. But I was a newsman with many questions that had yet to be answered. Most obvious was Muhl's mutilated hand. Why do that to a dead man? The answer was painfully obvious: Muhl was not dead when his fingernails had been removed, and what I had taken for a wolfish grin frozen on his face had been a grimace of pain and, perhaps, terror.

The next most obvious question was the noninvolvement of the American Embassy. One did not need to be a Hamlet to know the smell of something rotten.

An empty trishaw coasted inquiringly next to me, and I thankfully took it and directed the driver to my apartment on Tu Do Street. As I relaxed to the rhythmic pumping of the driver's legs, I thought sourly about Muhl's last prediction.

I had just killed another of his stories and sternly rebuked him for not sticking to the facts.

"Some day," he said, "some day you'll get involved."

I was.

3

RACHEL WAS WAITING for me when I arrived and together we climbed the short flight of stairs to my apartment above the tobacconist's. She seemed to sense that something had happened, but she remained silent other than the usual small talk one makes when another returns tired and dusty from a trip. It was up to me to tell her if and when I wished. It was part of the credo for keeping our personal lives separate from our professional lives. This really was a tactic for keeping the world at bay.

I inserted the key into the lock, flung the door wide, and stepped back to allow her to enter first. She smiled at my mannerism which she fondly called old-fashioned, but admitted she liked. "Cute," she called it, a term that made me flinch. It was a word that seemed to be coined to meet any exigency when other words failed.

Rachel stepped through the doorway and tossed her shoulderbag onto the table in the corner of the room. She crossed to the louvered doors that led to the small balcony and threw them wide. She stretched and touseled her hair and smiled at me, the corners of her full lips curving into deep dimples. Lines of tension disappeared from between her eyes.

I closed the door behind me and slapped home the dead bolt, a special lock for which there was no key. It was a concession to the war and terrorist activity at night. I collected the pole from the corner of the room

24

and turned on the overhead fan. I had no air-conditioning; after so many years in the tropics I had a distaste for artificial air.

Rachel slipped out of her wet khaki blouse and skirt and headed for the bathroom and a tepid shower. I headed for the liquor cabinet.

"More humid today," she called from the bathroom.

"The rains are coming," I replied.

"What?"

"The rains are coming." I raised my voice to be heard over the shower. Although the stream of water was not great, it drummed off the tin sides in a series of echoes that made communication a shouting match.

"By the way, my leave was approved. I have two weeks beginning next week. Is that all right?"

We had been planning a small vacation to Hong Kong for several weeks. At first, the plans simply gave us a common topic for conversation, but during the past two or three weeks the trip had become more and more important to us. Going on such a trip together would give our relationship a sense of concreteness as if we truly belonged to each other. I had gathered information on flights and hotels while Rachel scoured travel books she had purchased from the bookstore on Le Loi for things to do and sights to see while in Hong Kong. We were planning to stay at the Park Hotel in Kowloon and, using that as our base, take a ferry to Macao, visit the Tsimshatsui shopping area, the Tiger Balm Gardens, the Ten Thousand Buddha Monastery, and finish with three days at Repulse Bay.

I sighed, pulled my shirt from my trousers, and reached for the Scotch. I was about to break our cardinal rule regarding separation of business and home.

"We're going to have to rethink the trip," I called.

The water abruptly stopped. I took a large swallow of Scotch and waited. An angry burst of Vietnamese rose from the street, but I could not understand it for the voice spoke too fast.

She appeared in the doorway with her wet hair hanging in short ringlets and a thick towel wrapped around her breasts and hips. She crossed to the deep chair by the windows and sat. The towel parted at her hips but she made no attempt to cover herself. I marveled at the dimple of her navel while she lit a cigarette and leaned back in the chair.

"Drink?" I asked and motioned towards the bar.

"Explanation," she said. She blew a thin stream of smoke towards the ceiling and fixed me with her gray eyes. The large mahogany fan blades slowly swept the smoke towards the corners of the room. I finished my drink and poured another. I tried to remember how many that would make, but I had lost count. The number would have been irrelevant anyway for I did not feel any effect from the liquor. My mind seemed to burn with a cold, clean, white light in which everything was clear. I felt as if I would never be able to get drunk again. Rachel waited as I carried the drink to the desk and sat in the chair across from her.

"It must be bad," she said. "It must be terribly bad if you need a drink first."

"Muhl's dead," I said.

She nodded slowly and looked thoughtfully at me. Two tiny frown lines appeared between her eyes as she weighed her words before speaking.

"And you feel some sort of obligation towards him?" she asked. "Get me a drink."

Obediently I rose and crossed to the bar. I poured a generous measure of rum into a glass and squeezed a lime over the rum. It was good rum, dark and heavy-bodied, and needed no soda. I carried it back to her. A fine sheen of perspiration had appeared on her brow, her upper lip.

26

"You didn't answer my question," she said softly after sampling the drink.

"You knew about his death before I told you, didn't you?" I said.

She shrugged her shoulders. "The dispatch came through on the routine wire at the office."

"Routine?" I took a large mouthful of the Scotch and swallowed it slowly in stages.

"That seems damned perfunctory."

"I don't control the dispatches or their origins," she said. "I just receive and catalog them."

"Sorry. It just seems so callous."

"This is war. People get killed in war. That's part of the routine."

"But how could you consider our trip after hearing about his death?"

"That's part of war, too. Living." She stubbed her cigarette out in a jade ashtray.

"Besides, what's bothering you? You really didn't like him."

"That's true," I admitted. "But somehow he's obligated me. Don't ask me how or why, but I feel a sense of obligation towards him."

"For getting himself killed? That doesn't make any sense." She lit another cigarette and sipped from her drink. She casually tugged at the top of the towel as it threatened to fall away from her breasts.

"Perhaps it's just one of those routines," I said.

"Don't be cute. It's not becoming."

"I wasn't. Everybody has routines. This is one of mine. I am a journalist."

"Sounds more like an excuse to me." She finished her drink, and I asked if she wanted another. She shook her head.

"Frankly, I'm a little pissed. Do you know how hard it is to get leave?"

"I know," I said soothingly. "Probably as hard as it is for me to get a stringer to cover the office."

"Goddamn him," she swore softly. "Even dead he's an intruder. Why couldn't he have waited? Why can't he leave us alone? Damn. Maybe we should hang garlic around the windows and nail crosses to the doors. I don't suppose I can appeal to your honor?"

"That, I think, is why I must stay."

"I thought so."

"Sorry," I said. "I didn't plan any of this."

"I know. I know. The fortunes of fate." She rose and crossed to the bathroom. She paused to give me a kiss, and I ran my hand along her long legs. She was taller than me even without her high heels and was a true blonde as I was aware of, given the towel's distracting limitations.

"Where do you want to eat?"

"I don't know," I said. "Fancy or casual?"

"Fancy," she said firmly, deftly stepping away from my searching hands. "You owe me that."

She disappeared, and I poured another drink and carried it to the small balcony. The night was going to be soft and cool, a reminder that the rains were not far off. I leaned against the peeling wall and watched the people as I sipped my drink.

Things were so simple, I thought. Before Muhl, the war had seemed an abstraction that intruded into daily life on only a nine-to-five basis. For eight hours I would dutifully attend conferences held by nasal-voiced officers dressed in starched jungle fatigues, file the daily body count and usual glut of heroic encounters, dash off a color story on political intrigue or budding controversy, and join my colleagues at the Continental or Caravelle for a quick drink before meeting Rachel for dinner. There had always been a separation of time. B.M., that is, Before Muhl. When Muhl came he seemed to carry the war with him everywhere. He took savage delight in pursuing contradictions and political intrigues. The war was a tool for him to exploit and display his own talents and philosophies on the decay of civilization and decadence of man. I wanted to gag. Everything was becoming clichéd and platitudinous.

I finished my drink and stared moodily into the street. Neon lights began to flash in the dusk. Saigon had a few desperate hours to live before the curfew. Girls dressed in tight-fitting Suzie Wong dresses slit to the hip began to teeter up and down the boulevard on stiletto heels. Some waved cheerily at me as they passed. Behind me I could hear Rachel as she moved out of the bathroom and opened the wardrobe. I sighed and turned back to the room. A part of my life seemed to be over and a spark of resentment began to flare. Goddamn Muhl. I was too damn old to be a quixotic figure. That belongs to optimistic youth, and I was enjoying the pragmatism of the aged cynic.

4

AT FIRST, I thought the Chinese New Year had begun and exurbanites had joined their urban cousins and were doing a thorough job celebrating with fireworks. I was in no hurry to get out of bed. Although I explicitly remembered everything that we had done the night before and the vast amounts of Scotch and gin I had drunk without becoming inebriated, I still had a pounding hangover. We may not have painted the town red, as some of my peers were apt to say (old newsmen cling to old metaphors), but we had daubed a few shades of pink here and there in several saloons.

I sighed and rolled onto my back. Rachel moaned and curled into a ball away from me. We had made love when we returned, but it had been no good for either of us. We had downed too much liquor, and it was too soon after Muhl's death. A rift seemed to have opened between us, and I wondered if it was permanent or only temporary. It was too soon to tell, but I had a bad feeling that our relationship would never be the same as B.M. Before Muhl.

Rachel was shattered and vulnerable when I met her for the second time. The first had been a chance meeting on the steps of Lincoln Library, where she threatened to shorten my sex life when I tried to convince her to have a drink with me. She wasn't as haughty when I ran into her at Nha Trang after her lover had been killed while leading a raid into Cambodia. From what I could gather, Rachel and Captain Morgan had conducted a torrid romance whenever he returned to Saigon from the Montagnard village where he lived for six years while leading his men in counterinsurgency strikes against the NVA. Six years is a long time in war, and Morgan's luck finally ran out. He was killed while on a mission in Cambodia. Apparently, the Montagnards held a fierce loyalty towards the captain. Instead of burying him in Cambodia, they decided to bring him back to their village to be buried in traditional ceremonies ordinarily reserved for their man-god or chief. While crossing the border, they were mistakenly ambushed by a Special Forces patrol that thought they were infiltrators from the north, and the rest, as Edward R. Murrow used to say, is history. An international incident occurred. Rachel was brought to Nha Trang to appear before the investigating committee. I met her after she was through with her testimony. We drifted together like flotsam, each desperately trying to fill an emptiness: she from her lover's death, me from five years of living alone, knocking from country to country on *Times* assignments.

Our relationship was very casual, but we did have one ironclad rule: no demands. Our apartment was to be a haven and not an extension of the *Times* or MAC-V offices. So strictly did we adhere to our no-demand pact that it was three months before I discovered she had been brought up on John Wayne republicanism in a small town in South Dakota. Her plans for a degree in political science at the university fell apart after the death of her father, a shoe salesman, left the family penniless. The army seemed a better opportunity than selling cosmetics or slinging hash. At least it offered her a degree of equality.

But, I found, as our relationship matured, Rachel's concept of equality went much deeper than equal footing between the sexes. In some cases, she seemed a touch fanatic. During some of the liquid lunches with other reporters, she argued long and vehemently in support of U.S. policy concerning short-range Vietnam involvement. She was equally outspoken in her contention that the U.S. would have to recognize Vietnam as an independent country, once the current conflict was resolved, and not establish a puppet government subservient to the dictates of Washington.

At first, her arguments seemed idle cocktail chatter, but soon they grew in intensity, and my friends, tired of hearing her vociferous comments on manifest destiny and imperialism, began to avoid us. I couldn't blame them: Saigon was not a good place to discuss politics in public. Those who did only invited trouble.

Again, I heard the angry snapping followed by a muffled boom. Suddenly, I realized I was not listening to firecrackers and gay celebrants, but small arms fire.

"Jesus Christ!" I exclaimed and rolled out of bed and ran to the balcony. Carefully, I opened the doors a crack and peered out. The streets were deserted: the man who sold pickled eels from a cart across the street was missing, as was the old lady and her flowers. The stores and the shops were firmly locked with iron bars and gates over the windows and doors. Whatever it was, it had to be very serious.

"What is it?" Rachel mumbled crossly from behind me. "What the hell's going on?"

"I don't know," I said slowly, "but I think Saigon is under attack."

"What? Jesus Christ!" she moaned and grabbed her head.

I ignored her and continued my watch on the street. The firing seemed to come in ripples, a burst faintly heard followed by another only a block or two away. Once a nearby explosion made a fine powder fall from the ceiling and figurines dance on the tables, but the street remained clear.

I turned from the balcony and hurried to the wardrobe. I pulled a pair of khaki pants from the shelf and slipped them on and reached for a short-sleeved safari jacket.

"What are you doing?" Rachel asked. She still sat on the bed rubbing her temples, but her eyes looked clear and bright.

"Duty calls," I said. I tried to sound casual, but my voice cracked. I really didn't want to go out into the streets.

"Without coffee?"

"Very nice. People are getting killed, and you crack jokes." I bent to pull a pair of desert boots from the floor of the wardrobe and sat on the bed to slip them on.

"Sorry, but you've always said the smart journalist is where the fighting is not."

Another explosion shook the room and made the bottles on the liquor table clink.

"Doesn't sound as if I really have much choice," I said. "That was closer."

"Too close to go out," Rachel said.

"Maybe." I shrugged a nonchalance I did not feel. "But it pays the bills."

I crossed to my desk and checked my camera and bag. I broke open another carton of film and tossed half a dozen boxes into the bag.

"You're beginning to sound like Muhl," she said. "My brave Custer riding to the sound of the guns."

"Stop it. We'll fight later. Besides, that wasn't Custer. He stole it from Clausewitz." I got a fresh pad and two pens and a pencil from a drawer and slid them into a pocket on the side of the bag. I picked up my gunmetal flask and shook it: it was half-full. I slid it into one of the deep pockets of the safari jacket.

"Give me a minute," she said and rose from the bed. Her body was firm, without the waffled flesh at the backs of the thighs that most women over twenty-five seem to acquire. But I didn't care. I was trying to quell the butterflies in my stomach and find fresh batteries for my tape recorder. It was pointless to argue with her either, but I was aware that yet another unspoken barrier in our relationship had been broached. I wondered if I was seeing the disintegration of our affair or if it was being strengthened.

"Relationships are not unilateral," Muhl had said. "They are bipartisan."

I was drawn in despite myself. I think it was the idea of Muhl trying to be philosophical. I also wondered if he knew what "unilateral" and "bipartisan" meant.

"What are you talking about?" I asked.

He gave me a tiny, self-satisfied smile and leaned back in his chair and propped his feet up on his desk. We were in the office, and I was putting the finishing touches on the day's copy before dispatching it. The copy was not very interesting: Muhl had written most of it.

"Your affair," he said smugly, "was doomed before it began."

"Why?" I threw my pencil down and gave him my attention. It was muggy in the office and twin rivulets of sweat ran down both his forearms. He was not yet acclimated, I thought.

"One cannot build a lasting relationship on deception."

"Who's being deceived?"

"Both of you," he said. "By leaving each other out of your work you deceive each other. One needs to be wholly open about everything. Eventually, you'll find that you'll be forced into each's other lives, and that will mark the decay of your relationship.

"Of course," he added, "that will be a good thing, for destruction is often beneficial."

"In what way?"

"It erases weaknesses and corruption. It forces men to

rebuild and rebuild stronger civilizations. Each time man's dreams are shattered he rises, like the Phoenix, more glorious than ever. Eventually, through the process of destruction and rebuilding, man will elevate himself to the perfect world, having previously destroyed all useless things."

"Sounds Hitlerian," I said. "Another thousand-year Reich. But what does that have to do with Rachel?"

He waved his hand impatiently. "Don't you see? Man's affairs are but microcosms that reflect macrocosmic changes. What man does on a small scale—his reactions to affairs, his beliefs and the beliefs of others—prepares him for massive change."

"And is that why you are here? Is that how you see this war? Simply a reason for man to destroy himself in order to elevate himself to a higher existence?"

He shrugged indifferently and rose. He stretched his arms above his head, then moved towards the door.

"What, after all, is war for if not the advancement of man? The danger is that the right people may not win, and then a more corrupt society will evolve."

"And which," I asked slowly, "is the correct society?"

He laughed and looked mockingly at me.

"Don't you know? Haven't you figured it out yet? Think about the mandarins, Con. Think about the mandarins." He fluttered his fingers at me and walked from the room.

"I'm ready," Rachel said. "I'm ready, but I think this is great foolishness."

She wore a khaki blouse and loose-fitting trousers, functional instead of stylish, and a pair of tennis shoes. She slipped a small automatic pistol into one pocket, a packet of cigarettes and lighter into the other, and walked to the door. I wondered if the Truong Sisters had

35

been as casual. I slipped the camera bag over my shoulder and followed her. I didn't feel gallant or heroic, just a great fool.

We made our way down the stairs and looked cautiously around the jamb. The street was still deserted, and the firing seemed sporadic and distant.

"Well," Rachel said, "if we're going to do this, let's get it over with."

I nodded, thought about the flask in my pocket, and edged my way into the street. I kept as close to the wall as possible and looked carefully at the roofs and doorways. My stomach fluttered. Rachel nudged me in the back. I almost threw up.

Together we moved down the street expecting the worst. Nothing happened. Perhaps that was the worst, expectation. Action has a way of freezing time, and the mind, if left alone, builds horrors greater than reality.

"What's real about this war," Muhl had said, "is the opportunity the people have. I'm talking about the masses."

"Hello, Karl Marx," I murmured, but either he didn't hear me or else he chose to ignore me.

"Unfortunately, I do not think the people will get any opportunity, for the masses will lose no matter who wins the war."

"Self-contradiction," I said.

"What?"

" 'War erases weaknesses and corruption.' Remember?"

"Of course I remember," he said contemptuously. "But I also said that depends on which side wins. The true horror is the aftermath of the war, the fear of expectation, the vengeful nature of the conqueror. The terror of war is real and therefore not terrible. But what happens after the war? Ah, there is true fear."

36

"I suppose one needs to have faith," I said. He looked at me reproachfully.

"In man or God?"

"Both."

"Then what men and what gods?"

"That's the choice each has to make," I said. "That's your reality."

"No, that's speculation. And speculation brings terror."

"You can't lobotomize the world," I said.

"Maybe," he said. "Maybe."

"The streets seem clear," Rachel said from beside my elbow. I winced. Her voice seemed uncommonly loud.

We moved like last survivors through empty streets, past deserted stores, to Lam Lon Square. The firing had ceased, yet still no one moved. Almost no one, that is. Across the square Dupree waved at us from the terrace of the Continental. I nudged Rachel and pointed.

"It's Dupree."

"I wonder what he wants." She didn't seem surprised. I wondered if she knew more about Dupree than I.

We quickly crossed the square. Even though we could not see anyone, I still felt the threat of unseen eyes, imagined or real. Dupree was alone on the terrace with a pitcher of iced wine on the table in front of him. He was immaculate in his usual white, but his cane was different, a thick body topped by a gold ferrule. A Malaccan swordcane, I thought. Behind him the white-jacketed bartender moved slowly, silently, in the dark recesses of the bar.

"Will you join me?" he asked. He gestured at the rattan chairs on his left and right.

"Yes," Rachel said firmly and pulled the chair away from his left and sat.

"I really should try to get to headquarters," I said

doubtfully. I eyed the chair and the wine. The alternative was more appealing.

"No one will be there," Dupree said, and smiled pleasantly. "I'm not sure you could even get there."

"The Vietcong?" I asked.

"More likely the ARVN," he said. "They're very frightened right now and apt to shoot at shadows."

"Somebody has to know what's going on. Where's the fourth estate?"

"At the Caravelle. Or the American. One or the other. Perhaps a few are at the Rex, but I doubt that. The Rex could be dangerous." He was referring to the officers' club in the Hotel Rex, an excellent target for terrorists.

"Why aren't they covering the battle?"

"What battle? A few terrorists blew up the radio station. That is all."

"Were you there?" Rachel asked.

"No," he replied and smiled. "I have been here ever since the firing started. Would you care for some wine? It's sangria. Very cooling on mornings that promise to be hot."

Rachel nodded and pulled her lighter and a pack of cigarettes from her pocket, laying them on the table. She seemed to accept Dupree's word without question. I suppose it was the skepticism of a reporter, however, that made me ask how he knew it was the work of terrorists and not the forerunner of a well-organized assault upon the city.

He dismissed my question with a shrug and said, "How does anyone know who has lived the majority of his life in Saigon? One hears things here, a suggestion there. One just knows."

"Street sense," Rachel said.

"Pardonne?" he asked politely.

"I was explaining to Con how you knew," she said. "It is a term we use in America to expain how one simply knows without being told. It is like a sixth sense."

"Ah. Street sense. Yes. I like that. Very descriptive."
His teeth flashed in his tan face, and he poured two
glasses of wine without asking if I was joining them. He
noticed my hesitation.

"You may as well," he said gently. "There is nothing
to do for at least a few hours yet. Besides, it would be
very dangerous for you to go any farther. You will miss
nothing."

"I wish I had your confidence," I said sourly and
pulled the chair from the table and joined them. "What
are you doing here?"

"It is equally dangerous for me," he replied. He lifted
his glass and sipped from it.

"Gee. I thought you were waiting for us," I said drily.
I tasted the wine; it was cool and tart. Rachel frowned at
me and shook her head slightly.

"How did you get along at police headquarters?" he
asked.

"Not very well. But I think you know about that, too."

"Con," Rachel said warningly. "Be polite."

"I'm sorry," I said, and I was, too. After all, I was
drinking his wine. He smiled to show he had taken no
offense.

"It's that damn Michelin Plantation. Nobody believes
I did not send Muhl there or that I have no inkling as to
why he went there."

"I take it Trinh was less than enchanted with you,"
Dupree said. His lips quivered, but I did not see anything
humorous.

"He threatened to withdraw my visa and accreditation."

"You didn't tell me that," Rachel said accusingly.

"We don't tell each other a lot of things," I answered.
She looked hurt and lit a cigarette from the pack on the
table in front of her.

"Have you any ideas?" Dupree asked.

"A few," I said and sipped again at the wine. I turned

to look at the square. People had begun to emerge from their hiding places. The noise began to grow, and a passing cab backfired, causing everyone to freeze in fright for a second.

"It is over," Dupree said. "The vendors always know when it is over. Another example of your street sense. What are your ideas?"

"The most obvious is he was tipped off by someone who knew something big was happening or going to happen at the plantation."

"Like what?"

I shrugged. "I don't know. Could be anything. Maybe a major defection. Whatever it was, it was important enough for someone to murder him."

"Murder? That's very strong," Dupree said.

"And you didn't tell me that, either," Rachel muttered. I ignored her.

"Have you any proof?"

"The body," I said. "Bullet holes bleed."

"Maybe they cleaned him up before you came."

"They missed the blood from his ear. And there was a bruise on the left side of his forehead."

"That could have happened when he fell," Dupree said. "You really haven't much. I would be careful before I cried 'murder' if I were you."

"Then there's his hand," I said. I watched his eyes intently, but they did not blink. Neither did he ask the obvious question. He already knew.

"Do you have anything to tell me?" I asked.

"What about his hand?" Rachel asked.

"The fingernails were missing. Someone had pulled them out. Before he was killed."

"My God," she said, and gulped her wine.

"Yes."

Dupree still had not reacted. A tiny smile showed at the corners of his lips, and he began to drum his fingers on the table. The silence grew. Ice tinkled in the pitcher as Rachel refilled her glass. Dupree made no move to help her. Neither did I. She was the one who had wanted to stay. At last, he spoke.

"You, of course, have photographs of this."

"Do I need them?"

"Perhaps. Are you planning to write about this?"

"I don't know."

"I wouldn't."

"Why?"

"Because I do not have any proof. Nor do you."

"There's the body," I began, but he laughed gently and interrupted.

"Which, I understand, is missing. Undoubtedly a bureaucratic error."

"Will it be found?"

He shook his head and reached for the pitcher. I stole a look at Rachel. Her lips were compressed into a thin line of distaste. I suddenly realized none of this had been included on her routine wire.

"I don't think so," he said smoothly. "When such things are lost, they are seldom found. Will you have more wine?"

I shook my head and moved my glass away from the poised pitcher. My throat was dry, but I no longer wished to drink his wine. Rachel copied my movement. He refilled his glass, then leaned back comfortably.

"Let us suppose," he said, "that you are correct in your . . . assumptions, and Muhl was murdered. Do you have any idea who killed him and why?"

"Perhaps the Vietcong or the National Liberation Front. Or maybe the government had him eliminated."

"Why?"

"Because he got involved," I said. "He was too idealistic and had heard too many philosophies expounded by his professors. He was too innocent to know that philosophies seldom work. He never saw a dead soldier who was not a martyr. He was stupid and arrogant and voiced his opinions without tempering them."

"I see," Dupree said. He toyed with his cane. "You think, then, that his death was a political death?"

"I have to," I said and rose from my chair. Rachel followed my move and slipped her lighter and cigarettes back into her pockets. I picked up my camera case and draped it over my shoulder.

"Was his death political?" Dupree repeated.

"Aren't all deaths over here?" I countered and walked away. Rachel followed, and together we walked silently down Tu Do in search of a cab. I felt dirty from my conversation with Dupree. A young mutilated beggar stretched out a wooden bowl. I paused to drop a hundred piaster note into the bowl. Suddenly, I was angry; I was tired of playing the game: the plastic smiles of uniformed flunkies who parroted everything but the truth at official press conferences, the plastic smiles and lies at the presidential palace, the plastic smiles of the hostesses at the Americanized bars, the plastic smiles of all. What I wanted was truth, and truth was in short supply these days in Saigon. The war prohibited truth except in instances when large battles were won, and even then one had to look at press releases with a jaundiced eye. There was also the problem of knowing who was what. Everyone, it seemed, had "special duties" that were referred to by others in whispers. At least Muhl never spoke in a whisper. He roared like an angry lion, clawing and scratching, fighting to change the world. I had to admit now that his brashness had been somewhat refreshing despite the trouble he caused with his acid tongue.

"You aren't going to drop it, are you?" Rachel asked.

"No." I waved, and a cab slid expertly across traffic and pulled up alongside the curb next to us.

"Aren't you out of your element?"

"Yes." I opened the door for her.

"Then why?"

"Who else is there?" I climbed in beside her and directed the driver to MAC-V. She looked at me with pained perplexity. She did not understand. I wasn't certain I did either. Perhaps only Muhl would have understood.

5

"THERE ARE TIMES," Muhl said, "when you have to step in shit even when you don't want to."

I was drunk enough to think this very profound and nodded solemn agreement at Muhl across the table from me. We had been sitting in the Club Eve since eight; it was now ten, and the top of our table was littered with empty Beer 33 bottles. Rachel was tied up at the office and had called to explain she probably wouldn't be able to make it before curfew and would stay in the barracks. After I hung up the telephone, I moved restlessly around the apartment. I didn't want to stay in the apartment alone, but I didn't want to go out alone either. I poured a drink and carried it to the balcony and leaned against the peeling walls. It was early evening, that soft, cool time just after the sun has gone down. Down the street I could see the neon lights of the bars begin to shine. Here and there, tiny spurts of flame showed where vendors were closing their stalls. I finished my drink and wondered if I should have another. Maybe there was a book in the bookcase that I hadn't read or at least one I wouldn't mind rereading.

I had just turned away from the small balcony when something hit me on the head and fell to the tile floor. I looked down; it was a horse chestnut. I turned back to the street. Muhl waved to me.

"How about a drink? Bring Rachel," he called. He reeled slightly as he spoke. His white shirt was sweat-stained and wrinkled. He had a smudge on the left leg of his trousers, but it could have been a shadow caused by the light spilling from the stairwell into the street.

"Can't. She's working. I'm alone."

"All the better. Come on down, and we two baches will paint the town."

I winced inwardly at the cliché and considered his proposition. The prospect of spending an evening with Muhl was appalling, but at least we'd be among people. Here, I would be alone. Although I had spent other nights alone in the apartment, the idea of spending this night alone was distasteful. Why, I don't know. Maybe it was the softness of the night. Maybe the harvest moon. Maybe it was curiosity or melancholy. I went down and joined Muhl in the street. He laughed and draped his arm over my shoulders. He smelled like urine.

"I really didn't think you'd come, old sport," he said. "What do you want to do first?"

I shrugged and used the gesture to slip out from under his arm. A pair of *poules* teetered by on high heels and giggled. One looked boldly at us and said something. Her companion stuffed her fingers into her mouth to control her laughter.

"What did she say?" Muhl asked as they left us.

"She called us 'pretty boys,' " I said.

"So?"

"It is the meaning behind the words," I explained. He flushed deeply and looked darkly after the two.

"The bitch," he said thickly. "The goddamned syphilitic bitch."

"It doesn't mean anything," I said uneasily. "She was just joking."

"The hell she was," he said. "But that settles our destination."

"What's that?"

"A whorehouse," he said.

"Why? To affirm your manhood?"

"To wash the soul, to experience life to the fullest, to sing joyous songs inspired by dusky beauties," he said. He flung his eyes wide to embrace the street.

"What is the name for female pretty boys?"

"Lesbius," I said.

"Well," he said. *"Lesbius* see what we can find."

He laughed at his pun, hooked his arm through mine, and led me down the street. Two hours later, we entered the Club Eve. We had been to four other bars and had been thrown out of the last, The Casino, after Muhl dumped a glassful of ice cubes down the front of a bargirl's dress.

"We should have gone to Cholon," he grumbled. "To Le Monde. We should have gone to Le Monde."

I wondered if he meant the old Grand Monde, but doubted it: he was too young to know about the Grand Monde. He probably thought it was a place for whores. Then I remembered the Chinese opium den and realized that was what he meant.

By an hour before curfew, he had become pensive and philosophical, and I had become drunk enough to think friendly thoughts about him.

"I mean," Muhl said with the careful wording of a drunk, "sometimes you just have to get down and crawl in the goo with everyone else."

"Why?" I asked. He looked at me in surprise.

"Why?"

"Yes," I said. "Why?"

"For honor," he said. "For honor."

"Honor," I said, "is a frail word."

He nodded solemnly. "That is why it must be defended by strong men." He looked owlishly at me. "Are you a strong man?"

"No," I said. "I'm a survivor."

"Too bad," he said sadly. "Too bad."

46

"Perhaps," I suggested, "you are equating honor with foolishness."

"Falstaffian?" He giggled and hiccuped. "Nay, good friend. The word alone demands the sound and fury of Lancelot. It cries out for shining armor and white chargers and not the quailing mockings of one who skulks in shadows."

"Very pretty," I said. "But what does it mean?"

"You'll know when the time is right," he said and winked mysteriously at me.

He rose, weaving his way to the bar, and bought two more beers. He paused to throw dice with an American officer for the price. I tried to rationalize what he had said, but I was in no shape to battle enigmas. He came back to the table, having lost the toss with the American, and placed a beer in front of me, then sank with a sigh into his own chair and sucked noisily at the bottle.

"By the way," he said. "Could you hold the fort by yourself for a couple of days?"

"I suppose so," I said. "Why?"

"Need a little rest and relaxation," he said and grinned. "I met this girl at the Rex and thought I might take her to Vung Tau for the weekend."

"I see."

"She can do the most marvelous things, Connie. . . ."

"Don't call me 'Connie,' " I murmured, but he impatiently waved my complaint aside and continued as if I had never interrupted.

"There's this trick she has in which she puts both heels behind her head and . . ."

"I'd really rather not," I said, "go through a step-by-step account of contortionist love. It sounds like something De Sade wrote."

"It almost is," he said with relish. "It almost is. Anyway, can you cover for me?"

"Well, I don't know. I only did without you for fifteen

or so years. A couple of days one way or the other isn't going to make much difference."

My attempt at sarcasm slipped past him. He nodded and picked up his bottle of beer and drained it. He looked at me expectantly. I sighed and raised my bottle to my lips. I was beginning to feel bloated. Muhl nodded with satisfaction as I choked down the beer.

"Anything you want me to bring back from Vung Tau?" he asked.

"No." I belched. The room was beginning to weave in and out of focus. It was, I knew, time for me to go back to the apartment. I mentioned this to Muhl, but he ignored me and slipped back into his pseudo-intellectual lecture.

"The basic question," he said slowly and ponderously, "is if it is honorable for one person to solve the problems of another."

"I should think that depends upon the issue," I said. "Besides, one must be careful in one's dialogues with men. One could inherit problems one knows nothing about. Are you prepared to assume responsibility for another life?"

"The Caodists believe all truths are reconciled, and truth is love," he returned. "By that definition, if one loves his fellow man, then he must accept him as he is and, through love, aid him whenever possible."

"Again, very profound," I said. "But tell me, Muhl, what is truth? Not as a philospher sees it, but as a man sees it?"

He was silent for a moment, and I wondered if he had heard my question and was ignoring me, or had heard my question and was preparing an answer.

"I wish," he said at last, "you would call me Jerry. All my friends do."

I wondered who they could be, for I had never heard him called anything but Muhl.

"Sorry," I said. "But I think of you as Muhl. I don't think of you as Jerry."

"That's insulting," he said petulantly. I hastened to correct the impression.

"Not at all," I said. " 'Jerry' reminds me of the cartoon show with the cat and mouse. I don't happen to think of you as a cartoon character."

"You don't?"

"No."

"Gee. Thanks. You're a pal."

I almost added, I think of you as seldom as possible. But that would have injured him terribly at that time, and I was drinking his beer. If he wished to be pedantic, that was his problem, not mine. He was the one whose reach exceeded his grasp. But, unlike Browning, he, I was certain, would not be allowed time to finish his task. In the meantime, he would bore his associates with his vacuity and frustrate me with his repulsive prose.

We had another beer at Club Eve, and Muhl got into an argument with a young officer regarding the tactics Westmoreland was employing. What Muhl knew about tactics I have not the slightest idea. It seemed more like argument for the sake of argument. Muhl finally succeeded in sufficiently angering the young officer and was punched in the mouth for his troubles.

Consequently, we were evicted, and, as the time was close to curfew, I prevailed upon him to accompany me back to the apartment. I took him into the bathroom to fix his lip, and he passed out in the bathtub. I left him there, and in the morning he was gone. He left a note on my shaving tackle:

Dear Connie,

Appreciate you putting me up for the night. You certainly got pie-eyed, didn't you? Don't forget you promised to cover for me. Be a good lad, and I'll bring you something from Vung Tau. Thanks again.

Jerry.

P.S. I thought about your question last night. The answer is to set a thief to catch a thief.

J.

Another cliché, I thought tiredly. The sign of an under-educated man. I wondered. What was my question?

6

HE WAS WAITING for me when I arrived at the office. Rather, I should say, he was waiting for Muhl. He wore an old-fashioned, double-breasted white suit with wide lapels reminiscent of an old Alan Ladd film. The suit looked wilted and sweat-stained.

"May I help you?" I asked. I did not care for him. His black hair, combed straight back off his forehead, gleamed with pomade. His eyes were set too close together and glittered. Snake eyes, the old writers would have called them. The cliché was apt: he was as thin as a snake, and when I offered him a chair, he seemed to coil himself into it.

"I'm looking for Jerry Muhl," he said. His speech carried a trace of a French accent. Perhaps more in the rhythm than the words, for his words were carefully formed, the vowels precise, their endings pronounced in the manner of a very careful man.

"I'm sorry, but he won't be back for three days," I said. "Was it important?"

"To Muhl," he said pointedly. I caught the inference and shrugged.

"Sorry. I don't even know where he's staying. Or, for that matter, even where he went." I lied instinctively. This was not a man to whom one told the truth, since the truth established a basis for friendship.

"If you leave your card, I'll get it to him upon his return."

His eyes narrowed suspiciously, then opened con-

51

temptuously. Had I carried the lie too far? I concentrated on the bridge between his eyes, an old reporter's trick for avoiding one's eyes.

"Tell him to see Lautrec as soon as possible," he said brusquely. "He may leave a message at the bookstore on Le Quong Do. He'll be told where to find me."

"Sounds melodramatic," I murmured, as I jotted down the directions.

"These are melodramatic times," he said and carefully settled his hat, a crushed Panama, over his eyes.

"Don't you have a number? Office or home?"

He gave me a wintry smile and pointed at the message I had written.

"The bookstore. Le Quong Do. Will you see he gets that?"

"Yes," I said. He nodded and left. I wondered what business Muhl had with him, for he most certainly was not a bookseller. There was nothing studious about him at all.

I forgot about Lautrec as I busied myself with the old routine I had before Muhl made the bureau a two-man office. It was rather nice not to have to decide which chores to give Muhl, chores where he would do the least harm. By ten I had cleared the night traffic and made a neat pile of follow-up requests. I was telephoning MAC-V Information Office to check on the day report when Dupree walked through the door and asked if I had time for a cup of coffee.

The Information Officer on the other end of the telephone said Westmoreland was not scheduled for the conference, and he would send a copy of the releases to the office to save me the trip to headquarters. I thanked him, made a mental note about a bottle of bourbon, and hung up. I smiled at Dupree.

"The Continental?" I asked.

"There's a marvelous little cafe on Tu Do that serves excellent croissants. Gaival's. Have you been there?"

I had, but agreed to his suggestion anyway. I locked the door and followed him out into the hot sunlight. It had rained the night before, and the streets seemed steamy, but since the cafe was only two blocks distant we decided to walk.

We found a table on the sidewalk of the cafe, and Dupree ordered café au lait and croissants from the white-jacketed waiter who materialized at his elbow when we sat. He beamed at me as the waiter departed.

"So. What great secrets have you found out today?"

"There are none," I said. "Only old secrets with new men who think they have something new."

"That is a problem," he said. "And how many think they will succeed?"

"Oh, they all do," I said airily. "That is the tragedy of the individual: he believes in himself when others are corrupt. And in his purity from corruption," I added.

"And Muhl? What does he believe?" he asked. He leaned away from the table as the waiter placed saucers and cups of coffee in front of us. He set a plate of fresh croissants in the middle of the table and left.

"I don't know," I said, trying to remember the previous night. "I really, in all honesty, cannot say. He's an . . ." I groped for the word.

"Enigma?" suggested Dupree.

"That's it," I said. "But I would have chosen a synonym much less dramatic. Or, in the case of Muhl, melodramatic. Perhaps 'paladin.' " I reached for a croissant and bit into it. It was like consuming air. I loved it and devoured it and another in rapid succession. Dupree watched with amusement.

"Did I not tell you they were delicious?" He chuckled. "And the marvelous part is they have not been discovered by the military and been spoilt. I didn't know you were acquainted with Lautrec."

I hesitated in the midst of my third croissant and reached for my cup of café au lait. I sipped slowly and placed the cup back in its saucer and wiped imaginary croissant crumbs from my lips.

"You've been spying," I said. He looked shocked, and I thought of that marvelous double take by José Ferrer as Cyrano when he was accused (and rightly so) of loving Roxanne.

"My friend! You do me an injustice. I simply noticed him waiting outside your office."

"Was that because you were following him?"

"I was on my way to your office. It was just a chance encounter. I decided to wait until after he had left. How did you ever meet a person like him?"

"Why do you ask? What kind of person is he?" I reached again for my café au lait. It was cool.

"No matter. Just polite conversation." He pulled a fine linen handkerchief from an inside pocket and daubed the perspiration from his brow.

"Dupree," I said, "who is Lautrec?"

"You do not know?"

"No."

"Truly?"

"I met him for the first time this morning just before your arrival."

"I see," he said noncommittally. He fell silent and gazed at the tops of the few tamarind trees left after the army had removed their neighbors to allow for the passage of tanks.

"What does that mean?" I asked, irritated by his intrigue.

He smiled and lifted his cup of café au lait and sipped from it.

"Well?"

"I was wondering if I could believe you," he said smoothly. But his eyes did not twinkle to soften his words, and the tone of his voice told me that what he had said was not meant teasingly, but of great importance.

54

"Frankly," I said. "I don't give a damn if you believe me or not. It is the truth, and if you cannot recognize that, you're a damn poor policeman."

For the first time since I had known him, his face grew alarmed, and he hastily placed his cup in his saucer. He urgently leaned forward in his chair, his face a mask of consternation.

"Please!" he said. "You may joke of this at the Continental, but not here, not here. It is very dangerous."

"Why, Dupree," I said with delight. "You are a policeman."

"Not even jokingly, my friend," he implored. "It is more dangerous than you believe."

"Then tell me what I wish to know," I said. "Who is Lautrec?"

He sighed and quickly looked around. He watched a waiter clear a table close to ours until he disappeared with his tray into the kitchen before answering.

"Lautrec," he said softly, tapping his fingers on the formica top of the table for emphasis, "is of the Binh Xuyen."

I looked at him with disbelief. The Binh Xuyen, a mob of gangsters who, under their leader Bay Vien, controlled most of Saigon in the mid-fifties, had wielded more power and influence in Saigon than Premier Ngo Dinh Diem himself. The Binh Xuyen was similar to the Capone gang of the twenties in Chicago, except Bay Vien also had complete control of the police. The emperor Bao Dai granted him this power in exchange for monies needed by Bao Dai to keep up his expensive image as an Indonesian playboy. For many years, the Binh Xuyen had controlled the opium traffic, prostitution, and gambling in Saigon until Bay Vien decided to seize control of Saigon and the government. However, Diem's South Vietnamese paratroopers defeated the Binh Xuyen army and sent the soldiers running for their old lair in the Rung

Sat swamps. Bay Vien, with the assistance of the French, managed to escape to France. He was lucky: one of his cohorts, Ba Cut, leader of the Hoa Hao who had joined with Bay Vien and the Binh Xuyen, was captured despite having scattered one-hundred and five-hundred piaster notes on the ground in a vain attempt to elude his trackers. The one million piaster price on his head, however, was more than he could escape, and he was captured and guillotined. The Binh Xuyen coup attempt was broken. Or, so I had thought. I said as much to Dupree.

"Surely you are not that naive," he said. "Do you really believe such an organization as the Binh Xuyen, offering what it offered, could be totally defeated? We are speaking about major crime, not the pathetic gropings of your American Mafia. People love that which is forbidden, and Diem's catholic tastes and upbringing did not represent the will of the people. Although they applauded Diem's victory, they still enjoyed their indulgences, and Bay Vien knew this. He also realized his big error was trying to seize control of the government like your Aaron Burr. Unlike Burr, he had a second chance, and he moved the activities of the Binh Xuyen underground. And so it has remained, quietly, to this day. Do not be deceived! The Binh Xuyen still operates!"

"Then why," I wondered aloud, "do not the police take measures?"

Dupree cast another quick look around, then confidentially leaned closer. I could smell his bay rum and the rose of his pomade.

"Sometimes, my friend, it is more profitable and less dangerous to pretend to know nothing," he whispered. "It is true that after their defeat the Binh Xuyen who were left fled to the Rung Sat swamps, but Diem's paratroopers never found all of them. Bay Vien, their leader, was never captured. My countrymen helped him escape to Paris. He is like that Mafioso Lucky Luciano. He still directs his people here. Only now, they are silent partners in many enterprises."

"You did not answer my question, Dupree," I said. I took another sip of my cold café au lait. "The truth now: why is something not done?"

He eyed me carefully. For a moment, I thought he was going to tell me, but he shook his head and leaned back in his chair. He rested his hands on top of his Malacca cane, and once again became the broker he claimed to be.

"I am sorry," he said. "But I cannot."

"Why?" I tried to catch his eyes, but he kept them averted, totally secretive.

"Because, my friend, you are a newsman."

"Off the record, then," I said, thinking if I had a direction, I could look elsewhere for verification.

"No."

He was adamant. I could see that, and I sighed in exasperation. I could feel the story at my fingertips, but I lacked the lever to pry open the gate that protected it.

"At least tell me about Lautrec," I said. "What is his connection to the Binh Xuyen?"

"I am sorry," he said. "I have spoken too much already. Please. Just tell me how you came to know him."

"I don't," I said, my mind busily wondering who I could approach for answers. "He was looking for Muhl."

"Ah. That explains it," Dupree said.

There was a note of satisfaction to his voice, and I watched, alarmed at what I had let slip, as he stood and pulled a few piaster notes from his pocket and threw them on the table.

"What do you mean?" I asked, and stood and followed him as he began walking down Vo Thanh. I dodged around a tamarind tree and caught up to him.

"Mean? I mean nothing," he protested innocently. But

this time I managed to catch his eyes and did not like what I saw there.

"Damn it, Dupree," I said irritably. "Tell me or I'll let it be known that you are working for the police."

He stopped and turned to stare at me. His black eyes were flat and humorless, but I refused to look away.

"I am not," he said slowly and emphatically, "with the police."

I believed him. Why, I cannot say, but I believed him. But by that time, it did not matter. I was angry with his cloak and dagger prodding and angry with myself for letting slip the information that Lautrec was looking not for me, but Muhl, when he visited my office. Perhaps the people at the *Times* were right: I could be getting too old.

"I do not care," I said hotly. "But that won't matter, will it? The suggestion would be enough, wouldn't it?"

His eyes blazed momentarily, then died, and he looked at me with contempt.

"Very well. Your friend has been making himself unpopular in several quarters. To speak plainly, he is making a great deal of harm for himself with his questions."

"God save us from the inquisitive mind," I said sarcastically. "What do you think a reporter does if not ask questions?"

"I do not think a reporter, a *good* reporter, would be searching among the criminal element for news. We have enough with the war, I would think, to satisfy any crusaders or yellow journalists," he said vehemently. Then he caught himself, managed a smile, and added, "Perhaps your enterprising Muhl would do better to simply go to the authorities and ask them what he wishes to know. I am certain he would find the truth there and not with the criminal dissidents who twist words to aid their purposes."

"The question seems," I said, taking a stab in the dark, "who are the criminals?"

58

He looked at me severely, as if admonishing me for my heated remark, then touched the brim of his planter's hat in farewell.

"*Adieu,* my friend. I hope you find what you want. But remember," he pressed, "that there are channels for you to go through for your information. It would be best that you do so. Your accreditation depends upon it."

He turned abruptly and left me, striding down the street, elegantly tapping the pavement in front of him with his cane.

I wondered what Muhl was doing and determined to find out. But when I arrived at the office, there was a message on the office door to call the MAC-V Information Officer. The NVA had attacked Hue in force.

I read the message twice, wondering if someone was playing a monstrous practical joke. There had been no indication of an NVA buildup around Hue, according to one of my sources in Lincoln Library. In fact, the only war news for the past week had been isolated skirmishes by patrols who found the odd cache of Vietcong supplies in the Mekong Delta. Still, there was a special briefing called by Westmoreland at the U.S. Information Service auditorium for five o'clock (1700 hours, as the military so succinctly put it). I had something over five hours to contact the MAC-V Information Officer for a little pre-briefing information.

The door opened behind me, and I turned to find a disheveled Tran Am, one of my street informers, panting on the threshold.

"Come quickly!" he gasped. "Something of great importance will be happening at An Quang!"

I didn't question him, but grabbed a pad and pen and my Leica and followed him down the stairs. We raced through back alleys and emerged at the intersection of Su Vanh Hanh and Ngo Gia Tu near the An Quang temple. At first, I could see nothing unusual, but then I noticed a patrol of government troops with a prisoner wearing black shorts and a checkered sports shirt. His hands were handcuffed behind him, and his black eyes darted about in apprehension.

The patrol halted in the middle of the intersection and moved away from him. For the first time, I noticed the chief of police, Nguyen Ngoc Loan, and watched as he drew his famous pearl-handled hammerless revolver, waved the curious bystanders away, and without hesitation, placed the revolver against the prisoner's head and fired. The man grimaced, almost as if stung by a bee, then crumpled backward to the pavement.

Tran Am's breath whistled, and I felt the numbing awareness of death as I realized I had just witnessed a public execution sans trial and, as far as I could tell, sans accusation.

"I hope your pictures turn out," a soft voice said from my elbow. I turned to face Le Duc Trinh placidly smoking a cigarette. He gestured at the Leica hanging by its strap around my neck. A cold chill penetrated my stomach, and I looked for Tran Am, but he had discreetly disappeared.

"Did you forget to wind the camera?" Trinh asked solicitously.

"It was a bit fast," I said lamely, referring to the execution. "I've never seen anything like this before."

"Ah, yes," he said in mock sympathy. "But that is excusable, is it not, for you are a writer, not a photographer, and, therefore, unused to such stark reality?" He offered his famous death's-head smile. I ignored it and turned my attention back to the intersection.

"Who was he?" I asked sharply.

"Does it matter?" he said indifferently.

"I would like to know. For my readers," I added to make it official.

"Ah. We cannot disappoint the American public, can

60

we?" he said. "How would they get through the day without knowing a Vietcong leader had been caught and executed?"

"No name?" I asked, while busily scribbling his comments and my observations in my pad.

"No name," Trinh said. "He did not give it."

"Did he have a chance?" I asked acidly. Receiving no answer, I looked up. The death's-head smile was gone, and he was eyeing me narrowly.

"Perhaps you should ask your Mr. Muhl," he said, his sibilance emerging with venom. "Perhaps he knows. Is he not familiar with the Binh Xuyen?" He nodded a farewell and moved away, leaving me standing like a fool with poised pen. I cursed and closed my pad with a snap and hurried back to the office to get the story out. As far as I could tell, there was no other writer in the crowd, although I recognized Eddie Adams, an Associated Press photographer, and knew I had a jump on the rest of the newsmen.

I wondered about Muhl as I hurried through the streets (avoiding the alleys, for Tran Am was not with me) and made a mental note to question him thoroughly upon his return from Vung Tau. It was the second time in as many hours that his name had been linked to the Binh Xuyen. Unfortunately, more than twenty days would pass before I saw him again. On the heels of Westmoreland's five o'clock folly that afternoon, in which the wily general hopscotched his way around the question of Hue and played down the seriousness of the invasion, I played a hunch and hitched a ride on a supply plane bound for the beleaguered city. With the events in which I was about to become embroiled, I soon forgot about Muhl and the questions I had promised myself to ask. Afterwards, it was too late, and Muhl had made his ill-fated trip to the Michelin Plantation.

7

AN AURA OF the mystical Orient surrounded Hue when I first visited it during the French occupation. In fact, the city, at that time, looked more Chinese than Vietnamese. This is not surprising since the nineteenth-century emperor Gia Long had had the city reconstructed as closely as possible to resemble his patron's in Peking, even to the building of a mammoth wall to enclose the Citadel in the fashion of the famous Forbidden City. Inside the Citadel stood golden-roofed temples, palaces guarded by bronze griffins and gilded chimera, and carefully crafted bridges spanning quiet pools and streams. Ancient groves of banyan trees, sacred to the emperors, and mango trees kept the footpaths cool for the old mandarins who strolled their lengths while sorting out the issues of their day.

The entire city sits astride the River of Perfume, so named for its lotus-choked waters that give credence to the belief that the site of the city is the one spot in all of Vietnam where the white tiger and the blue dragon found sanctuary. On the exact spot, the Thai Hoa, the Palace of Perfect Concord, was built. I reflected as I stepped off the supply plane that day that any visitor to Hue would no longer recognize its bullet-pocked majesty and would pay little attention to the myth of perfect peace and serenity. A stench of death lay over the city, and the fear in the inhabitants could be seen by their pinched faces and frightened eyes and the apprehensive, hostile looks that followed me everywhere.

It did not take me long to discover that the military had been caught, in that delicious cliché, with their pants down. In celebration of Tet, most of the officers had been at an officers' party in the city's leading brothel when members of the North Vietnamese Army poured into the city from three directions, sweeping thinly manned sentry posts from their paths like rice chaff in the wind. In a matter of hours, the NVA had run up the yellow-starred Vietcong flag atop the Citadel and settled down to the grim fight to keep it there against the combined ARVN-U.S. forces.

From the balcony of the old French diplomatic residence, I watched the battle for the Citadel unfold as a sweeping panorama reminiscent of the carefully choreographed battle scenes in *Sands of Iwo Jima*. In the movie theatre, amid the odors of hair spray, perfume, and buttered popcorn, the horror of the battle was not truly felt, as it was here, with the agonized screams of the dying and the putrefying odor of corpses left too long in the sun. In the center of the square lay the twisted wreckage of a helicopter, the rotor blades pointing to the sky in abject surrender. A parachute hung from the head of a griffin, its cargo swinging slowly to and fro while the battle raged beneath it. Two men had died trying to reach the cargo, but only cheers met their deaths for they were the Vietcong, and the parachute was an American parachute that had been blown off-course by a freak gust of wind.

Mortar bursts rose in thick black clouds around the walls of the Citadel as a platoon of marines tried once again to breach the southern wall. They were driven back by fierce small arms fire, and this time two marines lay in the square like stringless puppets. One was dead, the other obviously alive but badly wounded. A sniper began to work over the live marine, beginning with the left foot. He taunted the Americans between shots, daring them to rescue their fallen comrade. A bullet struck the foot, then the knee. Another hit the outstretched left hand, and suddenly, a marine and two civilians were beside him. The marine leveled a long burst at the sniper while the two civilians awkwardly picked up the wounded man. A bullet struck one of the civilians, and he lurched but retained his hold on the wounded man. They raced for the safety of a low wall while the marine coolly planted his feet in the square and raked the Citadel wall with his AR-15. The sniper rose from his perch behind a chimera, then dropped his weapon and seized his breast and tumbled from the wall. The marine unleashed a stream of tobacco juice in the direction of the sniper, then turned and raced for the protective wall with bullets chasing his heels. He dived behind the wall, then rose and flipped a saucy middle finger at the enemy and disappeared.

I wondered if I should make my way down to their position and learn his name. But then I realized that would be useless. His heroism in the battle for the Citadel was the usual, not the rarity. Heroes were commonplace here; the unusual was the one who did nothing heroic. I felt their determination in the deepest part of my soul and wished bitterly, fervently, for fewer gray years that I might join them.

For the first time in my life, my perspective deserted me. I wrote long and glorious dispatches filled with colorful adjectives and accounts of bravery under fire instead of the dispassionate, terse, and cold prose that cut to the heart of the issue.

Muhl forwarded my accounts as soon as they reached him, foregoing his tendency to edit my work when possible. When I returned to Saigon, filthy and unshaven after the recapture of the Citadel and Hue, there was a congratulatory wire from the publisher of the *Times* informing me I had been nominated for a Pulitzer Prize based on my coverage at Hue.

"Goddamn!" Muhl said excitedly when I walked through the door of the office, wearily dropped my kit in a corner, and collapsed in my chair. "That's what I call writing. Congratulations!"

"Yes," I said wearily. "That was writing, but it was not reportage."

"You were lucky it all happened just before the Pulitzer nominations were due," he said, ignoring my comment. "This will be fresh and will remain in everyone's mind when it comes time for the voting. You were very fortunate."

"Oh, yes," I said sarcastically. "Very fortunate. Never have so many valiantly sacrificed themselves to further the career of one Con Edwards."

"What's eating you?" he asked curiously.

"Nothing," I said and closed my eyes. But the truth was, everything. I remembered the canals choked with bodies and a good friend, Stephen Miller of the U.S. Information Service, who was captured in the home of Vietnamese friends and taken to a field behind a Catholic seminary where he was executed. The Communists had gone on a blood bath after that. They raided the local medical school and murdered three doctors and a nurse, killed three priests, buried a Benedictine missionary alive, and gunned down any who were even suspected of having ties to the Saigon regime, including their families. Never would I forget following a marine patrol on a securing mission after the Citadel had been taken, as we entered the home of a cook for the leper colony and found him, his wife, and their three children bound with wire that had cut to the bone. The bodies were horribly mutilated with male genitalia sliced off and stuffed in the mouths of all. The wife and mother had been repeatedly assaulted by no less than, as the patrol leader observed, "thirty of the goddamned bastards."

Thousands of the citizens of Hue were missing, and it was hoped that they had managed to flee before the battle, but, contrary to MAC-V optimism, I feared a bloody purge to rival those of Joseph Stalin. The stench was horrible. Bloated bodies left lying in the sun had burst, and the rats and dogs and cats had been very busy with the unexpected feast left to them. Hue was no longer the City of Perfect Concord. The horror of a thousand hells had been visited upon it and reduced it to a smoldering shambles. The majority of the victims, however, had been civilians, not soldiers. It resembled more the unleashing of a terrible plague than of a battle, more an Armageddon than, as Westmoreland gleefully announced to the press, a desperate last measure to avoid defeat. Westmoreland used the Battle of the Bulge as an analogy, but I could see no comparison. Walking through the streets of Hue after the final battle was like walking through a slaughterhouse.

This is what I should have written, but didn't. Instead, I concentrated on the heroism, the gallantry in the face of an enemy who deserved no gallantry, portraits of apple-cheeked American boys stubbornly resisting the evil advances of Communism. I was the modern Ernie Pyle; I was a fraud.

But I did not explain any of this to Muhl, as I knew he would not understand. He was still too new for the truth, too fresh from reading glorious accounts of men in war written by World War II novelists, too caught up in the machismo of the fighting man, too familiar with the domino theory.

"I guess I'm just too tired for any of this to sink in," I said and opened my eyes and stared with loathing around the office that suddenly seemed a cell in a lunatic asylum. Carbons of my stories and second sheets were stacked neatly on my desk along with my mail Muhl had sorted and arranged in piles according to degrees of importance.

"Is there anything there that requires immediate attention?" I asked, and yawned and gestured at the backlog of correspondence. His eyes shifted to his typewriter, and he nervously fingered the keys.

"No," he said. "Most deals with congratulations on your articles and some requests for special features."

"Anything else?" I yawned again and ran my fingers through my hair; it felt greasy and my scalp itched.

"No." He drew the negative out and I knew something was wrong.

"You're sure?" A fly began to buzz around me, and I irritably brushed at it.

He took a deep breath and swung around in his chair to face me. His eyes were dark and serious, and the weariness abruptly left me.

"What is it?"

"Mark Tremayne died," he said quietly.

A silence filled the room, save for the buzzing of the fly I had missed. I leaned back in my chair to digest this news. Mark Tremayne had been the Foreign News Editor on the *Times* staff to whom I directly reported. He was the first to be promoted over me ten years ago when the *Times* pulled him out of the Singapore bureau, where he had proven himself to be an able assistant and clever news gatherer under my tutelage. He had a sixth sense for being able to interpret events and accurately predict their consequences long before forces put his predictions into reality. That gave us an edge over the competition, and together we had scored quite a few coups during the days of Sukarno. Tremayne's death meant that a position in the *Times* hierarchy had opened up.

"How?" I asked.

"Heart attack. I'm sorry. I know he was a friend of yours."

"Yes, he was. Have they named anyone to succeed him?"

"Not yet." He hesitated and looked at me. I could tell he had something on his mind, but did not know if he should speak. I waited, and he cleared his throat before beginning haltingly.

"Con, I don't know how to ask this, but . . ."

"Yes?" I prompted.

"It's about that position. Do you think I have a shot at it?"

I wanted to laugh. He had been in Vietnam for a few short months, and already he was ambitious. He hadn't even learned all the principles of reportage yet, and now he wanted to be an editor.

"I mean," he continued, and I could tell he was embarrassed, "they'll obviously promote someone from the field, and I was wondering if you would recommend me for the job."

There it was in the open. He hadn't even given me time to get cleaned up and relaxed before asking me to recommend his appointment over myself. I felt annoyed, but the situation was too comic for anger. In a way, I admired his brashness. Someday, it would make him a good editor. But not yet; he was too young.

"I don't know," I said. "I was more or less thinking of myself."

"Of course," he quickly answered. "I can understand that, but, well, you already have thoroughly established yourself here. The Pulitzer nomination affirms your value as a writer, not an editor, and I'm betting the *Times* will think you're more valuable here than you would be back home. I'm sorry. I know that's hard for you."

"I'm not suffering," I said, my annoyance growing. "Why don't we just wait and see what happens?"

"There's not much time," he said, stubbornly refusing to let the matter drop.

"How about a drink?" I asked and walked to the filing cabinet, pulling a bottle of Scotch out of the top drawer.

"Maybe a small one," he said. "I still have the day run to file."

"Of course," I said. "A small one."

I filled two glasses half-full and handed one to him. He frowned at the amount of liquor, but took it anyway. I got the impression he did so only to humor me, in much the same manner a child suffers the embrace of a detested uncle to get the present held behind the back. He sipped the Scotch and placed it by his elbow on his desk.

"This is a rather odd situation you've created," I said after I had tasted my drink and returned to my chair. "You're asking me to recommend you for a job I want. It's almost like a Restoration comedy."

"I wish you wouldn't think that," he said. He shifted his weight uncomfortably. "In a way, it's very natural. I think of you more as a friend than a boss."

"That's kind of you," I returned and drank deeply from my glass. The Scotch was good and cut through the weariness. I began to feel better.

"After all, you have been a great help in showing me how a bureau runs, and you have been fair in dividing up the assignments."

"Not really. There's seldom anything of importance from the five o'clock follies," I protested. Damn him for making me feel guilty!

"Still, they have to be covered, and other bureaus send their best men."

I wondered if, through his conceit, he had come to associate himself with Karnow, Halberstam, and the others who only attended Westmoreland's daily song-and-dance because they, like I used to be, were one-man offices.

"Somebody has to do it," I agreed. "That's why you were sent here. It frees me to do other things. I believe the term for it is 'expanded coverage.' "

He looked at me strangely as if he wanted to say something, but then elected to remain silent.

"I'm really not sure," I continued, "if I should recommend you anyway. You're a bit young, and you still have a lot to learn. Besides, I want the job myself. Don't you think that it would be a bit odd for me to recommend you in light of that?"

"You're being emotional now, not realistic," he said.

"How so?"

"I don't want to be brutal."

"Be brutal," I said magnanimously. "Cut me to the quick."

"Connie—" he began.

"And don't call me 'Connie.' You know I hate that."

"I'm sorry."

"For Christ's sake! Will you just say it? Short takes, remember? I think they taught that to you in journalism school, didn't they? At least they should have."

"They passed you over once years ago, and you're older now. You're even older than Mark was when he died." I noted the overly familiar reference. He continued, "Don't you think they might want a younger man who will be with the job longer?"

"I really should hit you for that," I said quietly.

"Don't try," he said calmly. "You're obviously in no shape for such playground theatrics."

His eyes reflected pity and, perhaps, a little scorn? I knew what he saw: a haggard, gray-haired man with the strain of the past days showing in the lines of his face, the sagging shoulders, and the beginning of a paunch. But there were years of experience in those gray hairs and lines. What did he have but his fancy education and a few years on the home staff as a rewrite man before being shunted off to this romantic adventure?

"Maybe my years will prove to be a plus," I said. I held up my hand as he started to speak. "I don't think, however, that you are ready for an editorial jump. I can't recommend you. If I'm too old, you're certainly too young."

"I see." He took another sip from his glass and carefully returned it to his desk. "You won't mind if I recommend myself, will you?"

"Mind?" I laughed. "Don't be foolish! Why should I mind? I just think it's a waste of time, but you do what you wish. It would help," I suggested sarcastically, "if you had something besides standard wire copy to your credit. So far, you've shown nothing unusual enough to recommend you for an editorship. That's what they'll be looking for when they make their decision, you know. Someone who, you'll pardon the cliché, has a nose for news."

"That's true," he said thoughtfully. "Thanks for the advice."

I grunted in disgust and rose, gathered my gear, and headed for the door.

"Don't mention it," I said. "And now, if you'll excuse me, I'm going home to a hot bath, a few more drinks, and a couple of days' sleep. Hold down the office, and I'll see you on Wednesday."

"Give Rachel my best," he said as I went out the door.

I waved a vague reply and stumbled down the stairs into the bright sunlight. I squinted against the sudden glare and leaned against the granite of the building to allow my eyes to adjust. I thought about Muhl's ambition and lack of credentials and laughed out loud. A jolly boy in tight chinos and silk shirt opened to the waist to reveal his smooth, hairless chest turned and smiled invitingly at me.

"Sorry," I said and laughed again. I turned and walked towards the apartment and Rachel. The thought was too humorous to dwell upon.

71

8

I WAS BATHED and cleanly shaven and on my third gin and tonic when Rachel, laden with packages, let herself into the apartment that evening. She stopped just inside the door and stared at me where I sprawled in the old overstuffed chair.

"Surprised?" I asked.

"Con!" She pushed the door shut with her hip, dropped the packages on the floor, and rushed to me. She fell into my lap, knocked my drink from my hand, and gave me a deep kiss.

"When did you get back?" she asked, when she at last came up for air. Her eyes sparkled with delight.

"About noon," I said and ran my hand down her spine. She arched her back like a kitten. I could almost hear her purr. "Miss me?"

"No," she said, kissed me again, and spun out of my grasp. Twin dimples showed in her cheeks, a bead of perspiration clung to her upper lip. "I have to shower. Mix me a drink."

She hurried towards the bath, shedding clothes as she went. I caught a glimpse of creamy buttocks as I dutifully moved to the liquor table.

"Have you been to the office yet?" she called.

"Yes." I carefully measured the rum and reached for the bowl of limes and lemons we kept on the table.

"What?"

"Yes," I said louder. I halved the limes in preparation for a shaker of daiquiris. "I understand I've been nominated for a Pulitzer."

"I know," she called back over the running of the shower. "Muhl told me. He also told me about Tremayne's death."

"Son of a bitch doesn't miss a bet," I muttered. I dropped ice in the shaker and vigorously shook the daiquiris. The effort made me hot, and I poured one for each of us, drained mine in a gulp, and poured another.

"Yes," I said loudly, as I moved towards the bath door with the drinks. "We worked together in Singapore around '56 or '57. He was pretty good." I kicked open the door and walked in. "Here." I handed the daiquiri through the shower curtain and sat on the toilet.

"Mmm. Good," she said and handed the empty glass back. "That leaves an opening, doesn't it? Back home?"

"Has Muhl been talking to you?" I asked, annoyed at the audacity Muhl had shown.

"Yes. I just told you," she said. She turned off the water and stepped from the shower. Water streamed from her breasts, and I felt myself responding to her nakedness. She reached for a towel and began blotting the water from her body. It was a trick one picked up in the tropics; heavy toweling made one hot again, while blotting kept one cool. I was beginning to discover it was also highly erotic.

"What's the matter?"

"He wants me to recommend him for the job," I said and raised my glass. "I believe he feels he has a chance of getting it. With my recommendation, that is."

"Rubbish," she said. She took my glass from me and drained it. "Why don't you mix a couple more?"

Obediently, I rose and retraced my steps to the liquor table.

"If anyone should have that position, it's you," she said. "You're long overdue."

"Thank you very much," I said drily. I decided to forget two daiquiris and began mixing a whole pitcher.

"Sorry. I didn't mean it that way," she said and

stepped from the bath. She crossed to the wardrobe and pulled out a silk sleeping jacket emblazoned with lotus flowers and slipped into it. It fell just below the tops of her thighs.

"I think you got a bad break the first time around," she said. "This has to be your turn."

"Perhaps," I said and handed her the drink. "Here's looking at you, kid."

"You do a lousy Bogart," she said.

"Bogart couldn't even do me," I replied smugly. "He had enough trouble doing Bogart."

"So what will you do if they offer it to you?" she asked, as she sipped her drink. "Will you take it?"

"Would you mind?"

"You'd be pretty foolish not to," she said. She avoided my eyes and crossed to the sofa and sat.

"You didn't answer my question," I countered and moved to the chair.

"Of course I'd mind," she said impatiently. "I'd hate to lose you."

"That's not the question I meant," I said. "Did Muhl ask you to talk to me?"

"He did mention he would be grateful."

"How grateful?"

"Well, he did suggest that he would be as grateful as I might want him to be." She grinned impishly to take the sting from her words.

"The son of a bitch!" I said. "He said that here?"

I looked around the apartment. It seemed violated, raped by Muhl's advances towards Rachel. I began to see our comfortable nest in a new light as a cheap, tawdry hotel room more in line with one-night stands than as a home for two lovers.

"Don't be so sensitive," Rachel said. "He's just ambitious."

"And ruthless, insensitive, callous, devious, and he

should be horsewhipped," I finished hotly. "I have never seen anyone with such effrontery."

"How about Madame Nhu?" she asked.

"Don't change the subject!"

"Sorry, but I want to change the subject. It needs to be changed. I don't want to spend tonight with Muhl, I want to spend it with you."

"You're right. He's not worth it. He just exasperates me so I can't help myself," I said.

"Enough!" she commanded. Then, in a softer voice, she asked, "What about dinner?"

"I thought light. I picked up a couple dozen boiled shrimp and some limes. Nothing fancy."

"Sounds good. And an early night?"

"Sounds even better."

"And we'll forget all about Muhl."

"Who's he?"

"Some whiskered gent from Missouri, I think. A senator, maybe?"

"Puns we can do without."

"What about my buns?"

"Lovely. Just lovely."

"Stop that."

"You know, we could eat later."

"Sex fiend."

"Yes, ma'am. We aim to please."

"Race you to the bed," she said. She stripped off the sleeping robe and leaped for the bed. I paused to shut the louvered French doors. Muhl had been pushed to a distant corner of my mind and remained there until about three the next morning. I suddenly awoke to moonlight streaming through the slats in the French doors that changed the room into a prison cell. I had been dreaming about Muhl. He had been trying to kill me with a rolled-up newspaper.

I rose and silently padded to the liquor cabinet and

poured a large Scotch. I carried it to the overstuffed chair. I watched warily until the sky turned gray, but Muhl did not return. Maybe it would have been better if he had.

9

I DIDN'T SEE Muhl for quite a while after I refused to recommend him for the vacant post on the *Times* editorial board. Instead, we communicated through succinct notes left in each other's typewriters at the office or with the bartender at the Continental.

At first, I thought Muhl might slip into a state of depression following my rejection of his wishes, but this proved not to be the case. He competently completed all assignments left for him and diligently kept up the day wire with statistics and uniform releases handed out to all news agencies by MAC-V and USIS. If anything, his work had improved. I seldom was forced to rewrite anything he left for my editing. Now and then, I had to tone down a piece that did not call for the flashy adjectives to which he had become addicted, but that was nothing unusual in a young writer. I had gone through that myself in Korea before a whiskey-soaked rewrite man had taken me aside at the Panmunjam Conferences and led me through a blue-penciled article of mine, carefully explaining his rationale for the deletions. It is a common curse that infects all young writers, just as gonorrhea seems to infect young soldiers.

It was just coincidence that I saw Muhl about a week later entering the 147 Club on Vo Thanh Street. I was en route to the office from a clandestine meeting with Tran Am, who had pieced together a route of narcotics that led from the Ton Son Nuht medical supply to the black market. It was a rather bizarre story in that the enlisted man running the line was using the proceeds from his illicit gain to support an orphanage.

Curious as to why Muhl would be going into the 147 Club, notorious as a gathering place for the prostitutes who had flourished following Madame Nhu's fall from power, I directed my driver to the curb and paid him off. I remember he was a bit upset, for the fare was much less than the promised trip to the office would have produced, but I ignored his protests and crossed the street to enter the club.

Inside, it was dark and lonely despite the sexual urgency that skipped around the room like exploding firecrackers. There is always something lonely about making a living through the sale of one's body or in the purchasing of love not freely given. The only exception that I found to this rule was an ancient crone in Hong Kong called Lisa Lee who enjoyed the diversity of sex so much she had made it her business and often delivered more than the momentary purchase warranted.

The prostitutes were dressed in Suzie Wong dresses of many different colors. The popularity of *Flower Drum Song* provided the identifying garb as a key for most of the young Americans who would not have understood the subtlety of a geisha or working *Dan Ba*. It was not the only time that American films affected marketing, but it was one of the most obvious.

A well-worn recording of Dean Martin's "Everybody Loves Somebody" played from hidden speakers while shaven-headed soldiers lurched around the room searching for the best price from the best-looking prostitute available. Two bartenders were busily pouring watered Scotch for the soldiers and tea billed as Scotch for the prostitutes. One of the prostitutes recognized me and left a young soldier for a moment to say hello.

"Long time, Con. No see," she said in pidgin English grown worse with American slang.

"It has been a long time, Phuong," I said. That wasn't her name, I was sure. Phuong, which means "Phoenix," was the name of the young Annamese girl in Graham Greene's *The Quiet American,* which was made into a film in 1958 starring Audie Murphy in the title role. Her use of Phuong was simply another example of identifying marketing. There were hundreds of Phuongs in Saigon.

"We miss you, Con. You come back for Number One Phuong?" She smiled and leaned invitingly against my arm. Her face was hard-caked with makeup to hide the deep pocks and lines, yet she still looked younger than the forty I knew her to be.

"No," I said and patted her gently on the arm as the soldier she had left glowered at me. "No, I'm still with the same one. But on the day that we are no more, I will make it a special point to visit my favorite Phuong."

"Ah, Con! Remember La Ronde and what you did that night with the paint to that French bastard who beat Ngoc Tau?"

"I remember very well," I answered hurriedly. The soldier's face was beginning to turn red. "But now, I search for a friend. A tall, thin American who came in before me?"

She looked around uncertainly and said in a vague voice, "There are many Americans here. There are always many Americans here. Has he a name?"

"Muhl," I answered.

The smile disappeared from her face. She looked at me narrowly and leaned closer to whisper urgently.

"He is in the back. A very foolish man, this American of yours. He does not choose his friends wisely."

"What do you mean?"

She shook her head and turned towards the soldier at her table. "I cannot speak anymore on this. It is too dangerous. But if he is a friend of yours, you should tell him about the virtue of silence."

She slipped in beside the soldier and, with a few quick and skillful movements of her hands, soon dispensed his sullenness. She was energetically licking his ear as I turned away from her table and moved towards the back of the 147 Club. I thoughtfully turned her words over in my mind. As far as I knew, there was no hidden meaning behind her words other than silence is golden. Still, the words obviously meant something more, for I had sensed the threatening tone behind them. I wondered what had upset her so much.

I found Muhl deep in conversation with an ill-dressed, scrawny Vietnamese with an ominous film over one eye. Obviously, this was not a chance encounter, for their table was empty of beer bottles or glasses. This, too, was strange, for I knew the bartender at the 147 Club never allowed anyone to occupy space without drinking. Socializing was for the park or zoo or with the vendors on the street corners near Vo Thanh.

"Hello, Muhl," I said as I neared their table. "Where've you been keeping yourself?"

Their heads jerked around. Muhl looked annoyed, the Vietnamese wary. I smiled at both and pulled out a chair and sat. I signaled to the bartender and yelled for *mot coc bia,* glasses of beer, for all at the table. A couple of girls began to move with interest to our table, but a gesture from Muhl's friend quickly changed their minds.

"Oh, hello, Con," Muhl mumbled.

"You haven't been around the office," I said lightly. I sampled the beer the silent bartender placed in front of us: it was stale and flat.

"I've been busy," he said shortly.

"Aren't you going to introduce me to your friend?" I turned to the Vietnamese and smiled.

"No."

"Not very friendly of you," I replied.

"This is private, Con," he warned.

80

"It is fine," the Vietnamese said and rose hurriedly to his feet. "I must leave now."

"So soon?" I asked with mock concern.

"Yes. I am sorry." He gave me a bleak smile, nodded pointedly at Muhl, and slipped away from the table. He moved rapidly through the crowd and disappeared.

"Interesting," I said, and turned back to Muhl. His eyes were furious.

"Damn you," he said thickly.

"What's the matter?"

"What are you doing here?"

"I was passing by, saw you coming in here, and just thought I'd join you for a drink."

His eyes searched mine long and hard, then fractionally relaxed.

"I wish you had waited a bit longer," he said. He reached for his beer, tasted it, made a face, and pushed it away.

"Why do they always serve flat beer in these places?"

"Those who come in are usually drunk by the time they arrive," I said absently. "Did I interrupt something?"

"Yes. It has taken me two weeks to find that man."

"Who is he?" I asked curiously.

He smiled secretly to himself and shook his head. "Oh, no, you don't. You had your Hue, this one is mine."

"A story?"

He nodded.

"What about?"

"You'll see it when I've finished," he said smugly.

"You know," I said, "the purpose of having a station chief is to have someone decide if a story is worth pursuing."

"Don't worry," he replied. "It is. You'll love it when it's finished."

"Then why not tell me what it is? Maybe I can help you."

"No, thanks," he said quickly. "I'd rather go it by myself."

"Muhl . . . ," I began, but he interrupted.

"Frankly, Con, I don't want to share it. You know why. You gave me the hint yourself."

Puzzled by his secretiveness, I shook my head. "You're speaking in riddles."

"Tremayne's job," he said.

Then I remembered. He needed something to bring his name to the attention of the editorial board, something spectacular like my Hue coverage.

"Oh, for Christ's sake,'" I said disgustedly. "This is juvenile."

"Maybe," he said. "But the story is not. It's good, Con, really good. And it's big."

"You'd do anything to get that posting, wouldn't you?" I said.

"I believe in Horatio Alger," he said mockingly.

"Then go ahead. I'll not stand in your way," I said. I rose from the table and looked down at him. His features were calm and assured. A touch of triumph glinted from his eyes.

"But it had better be good. Damn good," I warned.

He smiled and nodded at me. I turned and walked irritably from the club. Outside, I paused to breathe deeply. I thought about the Greek axiom: "Those whom the gods wish to destroy they first make mad." He was, I told myself, securely on the road to self-destruction. I did not know at the time how prophetic I was.

Soothed, I hailed a passing taxi and directed the driver to take me to the office. As far as I was concerned, Muhl was on his own. I was prepared to let him have his story, whatever it might be, as long as he did not use it as a reason to neglect his daily assignments. He never did.

For the next few weeks, he was a model reporter. When the story did not materialize in the next couple of days, I placed the incident in the back of my mind. When the Vietcong shelled the MAC-V compound at a tiny hamlet west of Tan Trieu, a small village just south of Bien Hoa, I forgot all about Muhl's preoccupation.

10

THE MAC-V COMPOUND was inside twelve-foot high concrete walls two feet thick that had been poured during the fifties to house a French garrison. The buildings inside the compound were large and airy, with ARVN forces occupying the old barracks and the MAC-V advisory staff, Major Powell, Sergeant First Class Jeffords, Sergeant Wiley, and Specialist Four Clarke, housed in the commandant's quarters. It was an austere bit of France with its red-tiled roofs and white-washed walls erected on the outskirts of a poor hamlet so insignificant that it lacked even a name. The military referred to it as Tan Trieu Two.

By the time I arrived, the debris of battle had been cleared, with only large patches of concrete missing from the bricked walls to show that a battle had even taken place. I had done my homework, however, and knew that the compound had a history of being attacked that went back as far as 1959, when six guerrillas had crept out of the dark night and killed two and severely wounded another out of the six who composed the first Military Assistance Advisory Group (MAAG) while they were watching a motion picture: Jeanne Crain in *The Tattered Dress*. The guerrillas escaped unscathed, a victory for the communist forces.

Since then, attacks had been made almost yearly, like clockwork, usually in July in commemoration of that success. This year, everyone was surprised when the attack came five months early. Normally, I would not have even bothered with the attack, as no casualties were reported by the Americans or ARVNs, save for an estimated seven Vietcong believed slain (it was the seventh day of the month and no bodies were recovered), but the senior noncommissioned officer had filed a report with MAC-V headquarters that Major Powell had been drunk during the battle and had been drinking severely since joining the group only three months prior to the battle. The army tried to hush up the situation, but a specialist I knew from a furlough in Hong Kong tipped me off with a discreet telephone call from the hotel in Bien Hoa. He had been working with the MAC-V group and heard the entire story from the group's medical sergeant the morning after the attack.

The noncommissioned soldiers of the group were understandably suspicious of my intentions when I arrived, believing me to have been sent to discredit their claim and clean the damning blemish of incompetence from the record of Major Powell. It was not an unusual situation for me, however, as I had encountered the distrust between officers and enlisted men before. Over several bottles of Beer 33 we came to the mutual understanding that officers did not work for a living, but were possessed of grandiose ideas that the enlisted men had to somehow make work, and it would be better for all concerned if the officers would simply go home and let the enlisted men have the war. It was the usual socialist argument of the value of the worker compared to the worthlessness of the aristocracy. It was an argument with which I was familiar, and, consequently, easy for me to express sympathetic agreement with the men.

I spoke not only with the enlisted men, but with the ARVN commander as well, a *Dai-uy,* or Captain, Dong, a nephew of the famous Colonel Vuong Van Dong, one of the brilliant insurgents who managed to overthrow the corrupt Diem regime. Captain Dong informed me Major

Powell had been a drinker of considerable portions since his arrival and had often drunk himself to sleep. He was, Captain Dong firmly stated, drunk the night of the attack and had behaved without honor.

My story was now half-written. I went in search of Major Powell, who had been relieved of command pending investigation. He was currently living in the hotel in Bien Hoa.

I found the elusive Major Powell, drink in hand, contemplating the Dong Xi River from the hotel terrace. His brown hair was neatly combed and oiled and he wore heavy, black-rimmed glasses that perched firmly on a nose many times broken. The nose and heavy cheeks carried a latticework of fine veins, and his eyes had the suspicious wateriness of the heavy drinker who works hard at keeping his addiction a secret.

"What do you want?" he asked wearily, after I introduced myself and sat down.

"Confirmation. Or denial," I said and signaled for a waiter. I ordered a gin and tonic and leaned back in my chair.

"Of what?" He drained his drink, held the glass above his head, and another waiter materialized, filled the glass with neat cognac, added a saucer to the small stack on the table between us, and disappeared. It was a well-rehearsed pattern.

"You know," I said.

"Yeah, I know," he said bitterly and turned his attention back to the river. "You're looking for more crap to flush down that toilet hole you call a newspaper."

"The truth," I said. "I want the truth."

"No," he contradicted. "You want to sell papers. You want distortion. You want a nice story about a drunken officer shooting the innocent villagers. Booze and blood bath. See? I can write headlines, too."

"What happened?"

86

For a moment, I thought I had lost him. His eyes reflected a strange, inner torture, oddly familiar like the thousand-yard stare of a soldier too long at the front who has seen all those around him die while he remains unwounded and cannot understand why he has been permitted to live with the enormous sins he bears upon his soul.

"Did you know this is my third tour?" he asked at last.

"No. Isn't that unusual?"

"Very," he said with a hint of pride. "But then, I was good, very good."

"Was?"

"After a while you lose it."

"How?"

"You go home." He paused and took a long drink. "Over here, you're a hero. Back home you're a piece of shit. People who were once your friends won't have anything to do with you. It would be bad for business, they'd lose the other friends they had, or else they really believe you are one of those killers who hack people to death with hatchets and string babies up by their thumbs over slow fires. If you do get invited to a party, it's because you're the main attraction like the bearded lady in a sideshow. And do you know why? Because this has become a very unpopular war, and the soldier is the scapegoat. They don't understand that we have to do this because we are ordered to do this."

"You could refuse the orders," I murmured.

"And leave what? Anarchy?" He gestured violently in contempt and spilled part of his drink. "You must have order. Do you know I couldn't get a mortgage to buy a new house because I was a career man?"

"How does your family deal with all this?"

"I'm divorced," he said softly. Tears began to run down his cheeks. "I will be, anyway. My wife filed the papers a month after I got here. She went outside one morning and found our cocker spaniel hanging from a rope tied around its neck dangling from the awning above our patio. They'd pinned a sign to its snout calling me a baby-killer."

"I'm sorry," I said atonally. I felt ashamed, yet I couldn't bring myself to feel pity for him. It was a familiar theme but not generally written, for the army tends to hide people like Major Powell. There is no room in a war machine for a sensitive individual willing to accept the responsibility of guilt.

"Sure. I know. You're sorry, but I didn't answer your question. Well, fuck you. I was drunk. Now, go away and write what you want and leave me alone. I just don't give a shit anymore."

He was crying openly by now, and I knew the tears of self-pity would soon turn to frustration and anger. I politely thanked him and left. I didn't want to be in the way of his anger. It wouldn't have done either of us any good. Besides, I had my story, although it wasn't the one I had come after. The simple article about cowardice under fire that had been indicated by my earlier conversations with the enlisted men was a pathetic piece of journalism compared to the piece I now had direct from Major Powell. I had discovered a human being who had become a victim of a government that had grown too large for the individual. People like Major Powell were no longer important. Politics had defeated the humanism of a simple society no longer a refuge for the tired, the poor, the huddled masses yearning to breathe freely.

The story began to write itself in my mind as I hurried down the dusty road away from the hotel in search of a taxi to take me back to Saigon. I was loathe to return to the Bien Hoa air base and beg a ride on a helicopter or plane. Somehow, the thought of doing so struck me as being highly hypocritical. I felt I owed it to Major Powell not to be hypocritical.

11

THREE DAYS AFTER I sent the *Times* my article on "The Decaying of America" (as I had titled it), I had an unexpected visitor. I remember the day vividly: one of those hot, muggy days immediately following a cool rain when the humidity and temperature combine to make one feel like a soggy piece of corned beef in a stewpot. The shoeshine boys and trishaw drivers were off the streets, and even the leaves on the tamarind trees seemed to pant for air. My hand was sweating so much in the heat of the office that the words on the copy I was editing threatened to run together in a pool of ink. I was irritated by the heat and the effort of trying to inject some form of life into the passive prose before me when a voice spoke from the door.

"Mr. Edwards?"

I looked up at a short, heavyset colonel in rumpled khakis. He reminded me instantly of Broderick Crawford.

"Yes?"

"I'm Colonel Black," he said and moved into the room and sat in the visitor's chair in front of my desk. He dropped a heavily scuffed briefcase onto the floor. His voice sounded like gravel. "Hot enough for you?"

"It's too darn hot," I sang. "How about a beer?"

"Wouldn't turn one down," he answered and mopped his face and shiny pate with a damp handkerchief. "Cole Porter, wasn't it?"

"Beg pardon?" I said, as I moved to the small cooler

where we kept bottles of Beer 33. I plucked two from the cooler and kicked the door shut. The beer felt warm.

"The song. 'It's Too Darn Hot.' Cole Porter?"

"I suppose so. Sounds right, anyway. How about a glass?"

"Bottle's fine."

Yes, I thought, it would be. I sensed a good-ole-boy, if I hadn't misread the southern twang.

I handed him the bottle and retreated behind my desk. He took a long swallow, smacked his lips, and abruptly belched.

"Onions," he said apologetically. "Should have known better than to eat onions in this heat."

"Yes. It is too hot for onions."

"Much too hot," he agreed and again mopped his face.

"Rachel—Specialist Holmes, I mean—works for you," I said.

"Yes, that's true. A good little worker."

I wanted to smile. Rachel was as tall as he and did not earn the term "little" by any stretch of the imagination. This meeting was beginning to take on the air of a Sheridan farce. He must have felt the same, for he cleared his throat and said. "We seem to have a bit of a problem, Mr. Edwards."

"What 'we'?" I interrupted.

He gave me a patient look of the type normally reserved for people who insult one's intelligence.

"You and I. It concerns an article you recently wrote concerning a Major Powell."

"I see." I sipped at my beer and met his eyes. They were hard and calculating, giving lie to the good-ole-boy image he tried to project.

"And what is that problem?"

"It's the type of article that could cause us more problems back home." He took another drink and belched again. The bottle was almost finished.

"By 'us,' I presume you mean the armed forces and

the government," I said. He nodded. "Too bad. It's the truth."

"No," he said, carefully selecting his words. "It's your truth."

"You're equivocating," I said. "Major Powell is a victim. That is the only truth."

"Not really," he said. "He's a man who needs professional help due to his marital difficulties. That's all."

"Your interpretation," I said.

"The official interpretation," he corrected. "Which is what we intend to release with a statement deprecating the yellow journalism that brought an honored and highly decorated soldier's private grief to the public's notice. We might even be able to manage something along the lines of invasion of privacy or some such thing."

"Bullshit," I said rudely. "No one would believe that."

"Oh, they would, Mr. Edwards, they would. Eventually." He calmly unwrapped a cigar and began to roll it around in his thick lips to moisten it. "Not all, of course, would believe it, but enough. And what do you think that would do to your credibility?"

"Come off it, Black," I said. "That's juvenile. A kid's game. I've been around too long to pay any attention to that crap. That went out with Grade-B movies."

He sighed and carefully placed his cigar on the edge of my desk before bending and lifting his briefcase from the floor. He grunted with the effort and removed a sheaf of papers and tossed them onto the desk in front of me. With growing apprehension, I gingerly pulled them around to where I could read them.

"I knew you would say that," he complained. "In fact, I told them almost word-for-word what you'd say, but they thought it was worth a shot. I'm glad you didn't fall for that old line. I'd hate to think a man who can write like you did at Hue would be so stupid."

I looked at the papers. The first batch, held together by

a large paper clip, was my article. I looked up at him. "This is carrying censorship a bit far," I said quietly. "In fact, it's close to constitutional violation."

"Not really," he answered. He retrieved his cigar, jammed it in his mouth, and leaned forward in his chair. "You see, that was given to us by your bosses."

"I don't believe you," I said. "I know those guys. They'd cut off their balls rather than suppress the news."

"I don't mean your editors," he said. "They never saw this."

"How . . . ," I began, but he interrupted.

"We went over them and showed this story to their bosses, the ones who look at sales and profit margins. We also made a tiny suggestion that the Pulitzer people might take a dim view of such an article by one of their nominees. You know how conservative they are. How large a boost in sales do you think a paper would make with a Pulitzer Prize winner on its staff? Maybe as high as ten or twelve thousand?"

"How . . . ," I began again, and again he interrupted.

"Let me finish. We didn't try to coerce them. We just pointed out the inconsistency of this with the Hue articles in which you wrote in such glowing terms of heroism and the tradition of the American fighting man. Why, publication of these articles might have considerably or irretrievably damaged your reputation due to the lack of consistency. The readers wouldn't know which Con Edwards to believe. You can see that, can't you? And if they can't believe Con Edwards' *On The Scene*, who can they believe?"

"I see," I said slowly. "So what do you think I should do with this?"

"Keep it for your memoirs," he said and stood. He arched his back and pulled the seat of his trousers from between his buttocks. He picked up his briefcase and turned towards the door.

"After all, the war won't last forever, and there will be a demand for the observations of such a man as Con Edwards, Pulitzer Prize winner. Thanks for the beer."

"You work fast," I said to his back. He paused at the door and turned. "I only sent this three days ago. How did you get it so fast? Especially since I sent it through Hong Kong and not the local censored wire."

"We have our sources," he said. He winked at me conspiratorily and left.

I leaned back in my chair and picked up the papers he left. In addition to my story, the packet contained five letters from the owners of the *Times* agreeing in nearly identical terms with what Colonel Black had said. I marveled at how fast they had traveled from the United States and how uneasy MAC-V must have been to lay on a special courier to bring them. Everything must have worked with clockwork precision: the discovery of the article, the five men to have been contacted and talked into mutual rejection of the article, and the entire package to have been flown back to me.

Suddenly, it dawned on me. I had forgotten the day wire on which we sent out preview slugs of news stories to expect so the editors could plan ahead what copy they would print against what space was available. Why had no one contacted me when the article failed to materialize?

I rose and walked to the clipboard upon which we stored the week's day line and budgeted articles and went back three days. I looked at the preview. There were the usual USIS releases on MIAs and KIAs, enemy count, dead count, a few short human-interest pieces on apple-pie Americans, the usual five o'clock follies on MAC-V's song-and-dance of everything's great, and Muhl's story on the squalid conditions of resettlement camps. I looked again: no mention of "The Decaying of America."

I replaced the clipboard and crossed to my personal filing cabinet and tugged at the drawers. It was still locked. I opened it and thumbed backwards. The carbon of my story was missing. I knew then how everything had been accomplished so fast: Muhl.

12

AT SEVEN O'CLOCK that night I was still brooding over my discovery. I was in a foul mood and had even quarreled with Rachel when she suggested that I could have simply misplaced the carbon. I *never,* I told her emphatically, misplaced carbons: to a writer, carbons were the crown jewels. Besides, the whole argument was academic: I knew what had happened to the carbons, I just didn't know why. Maybe my tone was a bit too brusque. Rachel took offense at what I said and curled up in a chair with a book, leaving me to sort out the problem alone. Two possibilities existed: either Muhl was going too far with his incessant drive for the *Time* posting and deliberately downplaying my contribution to the bureau, or . . .

"I want you to check something out for me," I said to Rachel. She put down the book on Hong Kong she had been reading and eyed me speculatively. The muscles in her face tightened. I could tell she was annoyed. I couldn't blame her. I had violated our agreement not to allow work to intervene in our life together.

"What is it?" Her voice was flat and expressionless, and I had a funny feeling it boded ill for me. Yet I had already asked the question I should not have asked.

"Is Muhl an agent?"

"I don't know," she said. "That's a need-to-know item."

"Can't you find out?" I pressed.

She sighed and snapped the book shut and tossed it

aside. She lit a cigarette and walked to the balcony and looked through the darkness to the street below. Bugs bounced off the shade of the lamp over my desk.

"Do you know what you're asking?" she said.

"Yes," I replied. I looked down at the papers on my desk. "Yes, I know what I'm asking. I wouldn't if it wasn't important."

"Why do you want to know?"

She flipped the cigarette into the street. I watched the red arc until it disappeared before answering.

"Ethics," I said. "What he did was unethical."

"How do you know it was even him?"

"Who else could it have been?"

She didn't answer, and the silence stretched into the room.

"I need to know," I said.

"Why? Because of what he did to you? Your wounded pride? What would you use the information for? To ruin him? Or as a club? Blackmail? Con," she turned to face me. "This isn't like you. Suppose you're wrong about him? Do you know what that would do to you?"

"I'll take that chance," I said stubbornly. "But I want to know if I'm working with a Judas."

"Judas? Weren't you ambitious once? Isn't there something somewhere that you did like a Muhl?"

"What's the matter with you? Why are you defending him like this?"

"I think you're being a little ridiculous about the whole affair. All you have is a misplaced carbon. . . ."

"I told you about that!"

"The possibility still exists that you could be wrong!"

"If I didn't know better, I'd swear that something happened between you two when I was up at Hue."

"That's a terrible thing to say!"

"I'm sorry."

"I'm sorry, too. The answer's no."

"Damn, I've never asked you anything like this before. But if you love me . . ."

My voice trailed off as she jerked to attention and glared at me. Her eyes mirrored her disgust, and I knew I had gone too far. I tried to retract the words, but could not. They lay between us, separating us like barbed wire, easily reerected time and again whenever we forgot what we had meant to each other.

"Forget it," I said. "I was wrong. It would implicate you if word ever got out."

"I'll find out," she said darkly. "I'll find out, and then I'll move back to the barracks."

"No," I said. "Please. I really would rather not know. I'll talk to him tomorrow."

"You really are an ass, you know that?" She crossed to the wardrobe and jerked a sweater from it and slammed the door shut. She pulled the sweater on as she went to the door.

"I said I was sorry," I said lamely.

"Shit," she said, pulled the door open, stepped through it, and slammed it behind her. I ran to the balcony and yelled at her as she emerged below on the street.

"Where are you going?"

"Somewhere. Anywhere." She paused and stared up at me. "Goddamn you!"

I heard the catch in her voice and knew she was crying. Helplessly, I watched as she walked angrily up Duang Tu Do, hesitated at the corner, then turned right, and disappeared. A group of old women laughed on the street below me. One of them said something in a low voice, and they laughed again. I did not need to be told their source of amusement. I left the balcony and shut the doors behind me. Crossing to the liquor table, I poured a full glass of Scotch and retreated to the over-stuffed chair and sat. I picked up a copy of William

Styron's new book, *The Confessions of Nat Turner,* and began to read. I had a hunch it would be a long time before she returned.

It was. I was over halfway through when the door opened, and she stumbled in. She was drunk, and I tried to ignore her misbuttoned blouse when she staggered to a halt in front of me.

"Hello," I said and closed the book and dropped it to the floor. "Have fun?"

"You know it, sport," she said. She weaved slightly, caught herself, and blinked rapidly. She is seeing double, I thought.

"Don't you want to know where I've been?"

"No," I said. "You can tell me in the morning." I tried to stand, but she pushed me back into the chair.

"I tried to find out for you," she said. A tear started to trickle from her eye, and she angrily rubbed it away with the heel of her palm.

"I tried, but couldn't find out."

"That doesn't matter," I said uneasily. "Forget it. I had no right to ask."

"No," she said trying to work her tongue around the words. "I wanted to prove I love you."

"You don't have to do that."

"You seem to think so." She hiccuped, and held her hand over her mouth. A shade of green began to appear in her cheeks, and she swallowed rapidly. "Do you know Muhl has an eighteenth-century copy of the *Kama Sutra?*"

Her eyes widened, and she ran for the bathroom and slammed the door behind her. Dimly, I heard her retching in the toilet as the realization of her words materialized in my mind. It was then I knew how a pimp must feel the first time before he hardens to what he is, and I pleaded with whatever god might be listening to forgive me and give me the words to allow her to forgive me, but

98

I knew such prayers were useless even as I made them. Nothing would ease the shame she felt for what she had done that night and the words that I spoke which led to that shame.

Muhl, I thought savagely. Muhl.

13

THE NEXT MORNING I dressed and left the apartment early before Rachel had awakened. Some things are more easily healed with absence, and I knew her hangover would make her detest me more if I was in the apartment to remind her of the night before.

The day promised to be a hot one as I made my way through the early market crowds to Muhl's apartment across the Saigon River in the Tam Da complex. It was a long walk. I knew I would be hot and sweaty by the time I arrived, but I elected to travel by foot anyway. It seemed a mild enough penance to pay.

Muhl lived on the third floor of a tall, white building throughly modernized by Vietnamese standards, which meant each unit had a private bath and a window air-conditioner in the living room. The air-conditioner, which worked feebly at best when it wasn't iced up, allowed the owners to charge more than the apartments were worth. This assured an almost total European and American clientele, creating an atmosphere of snobbery repugnant to me and a few other old Far East hands who still favored the old places with rattan furniture, louvered doors, and ceiling fans.

Muhl had just stepped from the shower when I arrived. He answered my knock with a towel wrapped around his lean waist. Water dripped from his bony shoulders and ran in tiny rivulets over the ropy muscles of his chest. I was even more self-conscious of my slight paunch.

"Surprise, surprise," he said upon opening the door. "I wasn't expecting you."

Had there been a slight emphasis upon "you"? I chose to ignore it and stepped into the apartment without waiting to be asked. He closed the door behind me.

"Why don't you make yourself comfortable while I dress?" he said, as he moved towards his bedroom. His bare feet left damp spots on the tile.

Obediently, I walked into the living room and sat in a chair facing the bedroom. It was hard and uncomfortable, a modern piece in chrome and imitation leather. I looked around. The room was neater than I would have thought, but lacked any warmth. It was more like a hotel room than a home. There was another chair, a mate to the one I sat in, a matching couch, floor lamp, small coffee table, and a small bookcase in the corner with two rows of books. I crossed to the bookcase to study the titles. The top shelf contained *The Rise and Fall of the Third Reich*, *For Whom the Bell Tolls*, *The Complete Short Stories of W. Somerset Maugham*, (two volumes), a couple of James Bond titles, an out-of-date *World Almanac*, and a paperback titled *The Guerrilla—and how to fight him*. A series of books by Tom Dooley was on the lower shelf along with Pierre Toucharde's book *Géologique de Annamese Cordillera*, Leopold Cadière's three-volumed *Croyances et pratiques religieuses des vietnamiens*, *Histoire du Viet-Nam de 1940 a 1952* by Philippe Devillers, and Bernard Fall's *Le Viet-Minh: La République democratique du Viet-Nam, 1945–1960*. Several pieces of paper marked sections of the books on this shelf. I was not surprised: Muhl was the type who would try to learn a country by mnemonics, a form of literary and cultural osmosis. I did not see a copy of the *Kama Sutra*. Perhaps he kept that in the bedroom.

Muhl emerged from the bedroom wearing a white shirt and trousers. He sat on the couch and looked at me.

"Well," he said pleasantly. "What can I do for you?"

"I want you to leave Rachel alone," I said bluntly. He leaned back on the couch and smiled faintly.

101

"I thought so," he said. "But I did not approach her. She came here last night."

"Just the same, leave her alone."

"Don't you think that we should leave that up to her?"

"No. She came to you after we had a fight. It was nothing more than that," I said. I was surprised I did not feel anger. The walk to his apartment had evidently accomplished more than I had thought it would.

"I see," he said. He pursed his lips for a second before adding, "I don't suppose she knows you're here."

"She may have guessed by now, but I didn't tell her."

"Will you? If she asks?"

"Yes."

"Very noble of you. What if I refuse?"

"Then," I said calmly. "I will ruin you."

He laughed, but his eyes narrowed as he carefully searched my face to see if I was bluffing.

"Do you think you could?" he asked. There was a hint, just a hint, of contempt in his voice.

"I checked Monday's day wire," I said. His eyebrows raised fractionally, the skin over his cheekbones tightened.

"And?"

"A certain story was missing. It turned up in the hands of a Colonel Black who took precautions against its being published. I wonder what the editors would do if I were to tell them what happened and that you were responsible for the day wire?"

"They wouldn't believe you," he said, but his eyes looked troubled.

"Even when apprised of your ambitions?" I shook my head. "You went too far, Muhl. If I were to let it be known that you had deliberately refused to move a story because it might have moved the limelight away from you, what do you think your chances would be of getting the *Times* foreign editor post? But I won't as long as you stay away from Rachel."

102

"That's blackmail."

"No, it's survival. The choice is yours."

He stared unblinking at me for a long minute before slowly nodding his agreement.

"Have it your way," he said. "But remember: blackmail is a two-edged sword."

"But it can only cut one way at a time," I said and stood. "One last thing: nothing, and I mean nothing, moves on the wire without my express approval. Just one thing moves, and I'll inform the *Times*. I hope I've been succinct. We'll work together, but that's it. I do not want to see you otherwise. Understood?"

"Understood," he said quietly.

"Good," I replied and walked to the door. "I'll leave your assignments on the desk. But remember: I want to see them before you send them."

I paused at the door, my hand upon the doorknob. "You know, I have met a lot of conniving bastards in this business, but you are the cheapest son of a bitch I have ever met."

I opened the door and departed, leaving it for him to close. I could feel the anger beginning to return as I walked down the stairs into the hot sunlight. I knew that Muhl had won despite my threat. He had successfully blocked my story and gotten away with it. He had even managed to take Rachel from me. I had only managed to insure that he would not do that again, but it was only a minor triumph while he had won the major victory. He would, however, be hard-pressed to make a further name for himself. I was thoroughly resolved to limit him to routine only at the office. The feature stories, the plums that would have brought his name to the attention of the *Times* editors, I would do myself. He would remember his assignment here as one in which he had had no chance to further his career. That was, I thought, the worst thing I could do to him. I would rob him of that which he held most dear: time.

14

THE DAYS QUICKLY settled into a routine, for which I was grateful. Routine is a soothing balm to ease life's unpleasantries. It allows time to pass quickly and heal the wounds. The thoughts of Muhl and Rachel were pushed to the back of my mind by the USIS bulletin, attacks on Special Forces camps, and conflicting reports from the Saigon government regarding the state of the war. I left Muhl the chore of covering the briefings on statistics and assigned him the mediocre stories such as the increase of prostitution and the various assignments of army personnel. I allowed him to cover certain pacification programs, such as the building of schools in outlying hamlets and the movements of supplies, but nothing that would allow him more than five paragraphs or "fillers," as they were called by editors who could use them to complete a column of copy in the newspaper. His byline was conspicuously absent from stories.

Slowly, things returned to a semblance of normality between Rachel and me. We did not talk about that night and seldom went out to our old haunts, to keep from running into Muhl. Still, there seemed to be a barrier between us, and we found ourselves quarreling over petty things that before Muhl we would have ignored.

On the night of her birthday, I took her to the Mekong Floating Restaurant for dinner. We met a Special Forces captain from Plei Me we had become acquainted with once in Nha Trang and invited him to join us. After many Scotches and a bottle of champagne, he hinted that it

104

would be a good idea for me to fly back with him and check out what he called "discrepancies" in reports released by MAC-V to the press.

At first, I demurred, but as the evening progressed and Rachel became moody and depressed about being a year older (she had just turned thirty), I decided it might be a good idea after all. By the time I returned, she would have grown used to her age. I also placed a lot of value in the old cliché about absences and hearts and promised Rachel to take her to Hong Kong upon my return. That seemed to cheer her up a bit, and we spent the rest of the night dancing at the old Grande Monde in Cholon and drinking illegal Chinese brandy.

A special press plane was due to leave in the morning for Nha Trang, and I had scheduled Muhl for it, as the program involved a party for a sergeant who had been promoted to warrant officer in the transportation corps. Such a promotion was unusual enough to indicate a little coverage. Before making the assignment, I considered it a way to get Muhl out of my hair for a couple of days. But now I decided to take the plane and meet the captain in Nha Trang and hitch a ride with him to Plei Me. Muhl would once again be assigned to the USIS briefings.

He did not look happy when I informed him about the change in plans the next day at the office, though he did not protest. He seemed resigned to his fate. I warned him not to send anything out over the wire except for the usual releases from MAC-V and USIS and to leave a copy of each day wire on my desk so I could check it upon my return.

The last I saw of Muhl, he was sitting at his desk and separating second carbons for filing and follow-up. When I returned from Plei Me and Nha Trang, he was dead.

15

THE ATTACK ON the radio station was played down by MAC-V as the work of isolated terrorists acting on their own and was not, Captain Fleming, the Information Officer, emphasized, the result of a planned NVA probe. Casualties were light and mostly ARVN soldiers. The terrorists had elected to die rather than surrender, and no retaliatory measures were planned.

Where, I wondered, would the attacks have been made and against whom if retaliation had been planned? However, I kept this point to myself, for I wanted to get back to the office and file the stories in time to make deadline back in the States. My impatience almost made me careless and would have if anybody but Ed Logan had asked the question.

"Will General Westmoreland ask for more soldiers from the president to insure against this happening again?"

Captain Fleming frowned and shook his head at Logan's question and repeated himself: "No. As I stated before, this was just an isolated case of terrorism."

"How does the military know this to be an isolated form of terrorism?"

"We have information from, ah, outside sources to confirm this."

"What sources?" Logan asked.

"I'm not at liberty to say. That is a confidential matter."

106

"What . . . ," began another correspondent, but Logan cut him off.

"Can you define 'terrorism' for us, Captain? That is, how the military differentiates between 'terrorism' and the non-terrorist attacks?"

"I don't believe terrorism needs to be defined," Captain Fleming said stiffly. "At least, not for such an experienced press corps as this."

"Humor me," Logan said nastily. "Define a terrorist."

"Very well. A terrorist is one who engages, without military sanction or guidances, targets which he feels will give him the optimum press for his political or apolitical beliefs, usually to the extreme left or right, and more for their demoralizing and dramatic effect than for their intrinsic military value."

"There is no military value to their targets?"

"No."

"Would you consider a radio station a military target?"

"If used for propaganda purposes, but in this case, other targets should have been selected to insure the seizure of the radio station would succeed. That is one of the reasons why we know the attacks to have been of terrorist origin rather than military."

Logan smiled benignly and rocked back on his heels as he glanced at the notepad in his hand.

"Tell us, Captain, by your definition of a terrorist, are not the Vietcong terrorists?"

"No." Captain Fleming looked annoyed. He began to shuffle the papers on the podium in front of him. I knew those papers contained the dry facts and figures on dead and wounded that the army usually released at this time. Ordinarily, the press would have taken these and run, after a few perfunctory comments and observations that had little worth as news, but were dutifully reported to be used as fillers.

"The Vietcong are guerrillas who perform a military function with attacks on military targets or are used in isolated attacks to harass the enemy in isolated areas outside war zones."

"Are not these harassing attacks similar to terrorist attacks? Do they not accomplish the same thing? Disruption of order?"

"Yes," Captain Fleming said grudgingly. He did not like the turn Logan's questions were taking. They were far off the briefing he had planned. He pointedly shuffled the papers again.

"Which brings us back to the original question," Logan said smoothly. "How does the military know this recent attack on Saigon to have been made by terrorists and not the Vietcong? Or, for that matter, the NVA?"

"I told you we have outside information," the Captain snapped. "For security reasons, I cannot identify sources any further."

"Are you implying the existence of something besides the Vietcong and the NVA?"

"I am implying nothing," Captain Fleming said. "And now, I'm afraid I'll have to close this briefing. You will find prepared statements for you at the rear of the auditorium. Thank you for your patience."

He placed a slight emphasis on "patience" and frowned at Logan, who smiled benignly at him and bent his head to scribble in his notepad.

The captain gathered his papers, nodded at us, and strode quickly from the platform. A young specialist who had been taking notes to the left of the platform smiled broadly at Logan and hurried after the captain.

I stretched and waited as the other members of the press moved to the back of the auditorium to pick up blue mimeographed copies of the papers the captain had been so eager to read to us. I walked over to Logan and congratulated him for being such an adroit devil's advocate.

"I did get that mental midget hopping around, didn't I?" he said smugly. "For a minute there, I thought we might actually get something we could use."

"Why do you suppose he was so evasive?"

"You mean his 'outside sources'?"

"Yes. Do you think they could have been nonmilitary?"

"Like what?" He paused and looked shrewdly at me. "You working on something you'd care to share, old buddy?"

"No," I said slowly. "Just curious."

"There's another way of looking at it, too," he said meditatively. "Maybe he just doesn't know."

"Then why not say so?"

"And look a fool?" Logan laughed. "Do you know any young captain who would take such a gamble?"

"No," I said. A thought was beginning to materialize in my mind. "No, you're right, of course. It just seems strange to me."

"Be careful, old buddy," he said and slapped me on the shoulder. "You're beginning to sound a bit paranoid."

"It goes with the territory," I automatically replied and moved with him to the rear of the auditorium to pick up a copy of the day's briefing for the day wire.

We parted company outside after making a date for drinks later that evening at the Continental. He hurried away to file the statistics we had been given and write a perfunctory cover story to follow them. I watched his back disappear through the crowd and turned towards my office. I stopped. A white-coated figure was watching me from a doorway. He noticed my attention and quickly turned and slipped into the shop.

I moved slowly down the street. I couldn't be sure, for his face had been in shadow, but somehow I knew the figure had been Lautrec, and his presence outside the USIS did not make any sense. People like Lautrec make it a point to keep a low profile. Something important made him take the chance of being seen and recognized. The idea that had started to germinate in my mind in the auditorium continued to grow as I remembered my conversation with Dupree at Gaival's before Muhl was killed.

I increased my pace towards the office. I was impatient to file the day wire and find Dupree. I had a few more questions for him regarding the Binh Xuyen.

16

DUPREE WAS SITTING at a table on the terrace of the Continental placidly sipping absinthe and reading the latest copy of the *Times* when I found him. I pulled a chair out from the table, sat opposite him, and beckoned to the waiter. Dupree raised his eyebrow at my lack of manners, but commented only on Muhl's eulogy.

"I have just been reading your . . . ," he frowned as he searched for the correct word, "eulogy? Very good. One would think you and Muhl were the closest of friends."

He neatly folded the paper and placed it beside his glass and reached for his absinthe. He sipped it delicately. The waiter appeared and I ordered a gin and tonic and another absinthe for Dupree. He gracefully nodded his appreciation and tapped the folded paper with a manicured nail as the waiter left.

"You have captured the essence of the man without blackly painting him as he truly was. That is very good, very good indeed, considering how you felt towards him."

"One does not speak ill of the dead," I admonished. "The first rule of journalism: all the dead are saints."

He laughed and relaxed against the chair back. He removed a polished silver cigarette case from an inside pocket of his coat and critically selected a Gauloise.

"It must have been very hard for you to write," he said sympathetically. He lit the cigarette with a Swan.

"I deal with lies every day," I said. "After a while, one gets used to making the lies read like gray truth."

" 'Gray truth.' I must remember that." He blew a cloud of smoke into the air and stared past it at the square. "Of course, Zola would not have approved."

"No," I agreed. "But Zola would not have recognized the existence of a higher truth."

"There is a truth higher than truth? Do you not remember *J'accuse?*"

"I remember. But Zola was too concerned with truth for truth's sake. He forgot survival. In the end, that killed him."

"His death was an accident," Dupree objected.

"Was it?" I murmured. "He had many political enemies, *violent* enemies."

Dupree nodded thoughtfully. "The question, of course, is whether life is preferable to honor. That is . . ."

I interrupted. "Honor belongs to the individual and, therefore, is an intimate aspect of life, so kindly keep your nose out of my life. I live it the way I choose."

He did not take offense, but smiled indulgently at me. "You may hope to live as you wish, but are you?"

"Theosophy is the opiate of the idle," I said. "I came to ask you a couple of questions."

"I am honored," he said. The waiter appeared with our order. We waited as he silently cleaned the table and placed our drinks in front of us. One of the charming traditions the Continental adhered to was the use of saucers rather than flimsy napkins with cute jokes written upon them as coasters for glasses. Only two other bars that I knew of still used saucers: the bar at the hotel in Bien Hoa and Raffles in Singapore. It was a relaxing, old-world nostalgia that soothed me and gave me an anchor in a hectic world. Dupree, however, did not share my feelings.

"The Continental still does not enter the sixties," he said critically. He daintily dabbed his upper lip with a scented handkerchief. "But, then, that does give one a sense of security." He lifted his glass to his lips.

112

"Security is an illusion," I said. "What can you tell me about the Binh Xuyen?"

There was only the slightest hesitation between the rim of the glass and his lips. He thoughtfully sipped the absinthe and replaced the glass onto the saucer and again dabbed his lips.

"Nothing more than anyone else," he said smoothly. "It is all a matter of public record. In fact, I do believe you wrote a series of definitive articles about the Binh Xuyen in the mid-fifties when Bay Vien decided to oust Diem from the government. Yes, I remember now: 'Against a gray dawn, mortars cracked and machine guns spat their staccato death as the Binh Xuyen moved against government troops in a fierce bid to seize the Boulevard Gallieni . . .' Very colorful prose."

"Thank you," I said sarcastically. "But I remember *then*, what I want is *now*."

"Now?" He raised his eyebrows in pretended puzzlement. "But if you remember your words, then surely you remember the Binh Xuyen was defeated."

"Dupree," I said patiently. "Don't insult my intelligence. Crime is a floating passion of the people: it can never be erased."

"Very astute. Clichéd, but very astute. Incidentally, have you ever noticed that all the great writers often spoke in clichés?"

"Clichés," I said impatiently, "are often very handy. They save words because everyone understands them. You're evading me."

He sighed and fixed a steady gaze upon me. His eyes were indolent, but steady and guarded.

"What is it you wish?"

"Lautrec," I said promptly. "I wish to speak with Lautrec."

"And what makes you think I might be able to help you?"

I did not answer him, but gave him what I hoped was a

113

hard and piercing look. He met my stare for a moment, then his eyes shifted to the square.

"I am only . . . ," he began, but again I interrupted. I was determined not to give him an escape.

"I know what you are. You confirmed my suspicions at Gaival's when I first asked you about Lautrec."

"Yes," he said. He lifted his glass and thoughtfully sipped from it. "I was rather careless, but there were reasons for my carelessness."

"I do not need to hear them," I said. "Lautrec?"

He sighed and shifted his position in his chair. His fingers drummed for a moment upon the folded newspaper, then stopped.

"This will be off-the-record, as you Americans put it?"

I shrugged and elaborately lifted my gin and tonic, tasted it, and set it back into its saucer.

"You know better than that," I said. " 'Off-the-record' is for historians or journalism neophytes."

He obviously did not like the open door I refused to shut. He wanted some sense of security, and I knew if he wanted that, what he could tell me was very, very important. Men like Dupree enjoy a hint of danger, but real danger makes them uneasy and wary.

"Lautrec," he said slowly, "is the *Nghi-si* of the Binh Xuyen. He is the Saigon controller for Bay Vien. More like a laicist, I suppose, who divides his time between Vien's forces in the Rung Sat swamps and here. Lautrec manages to keep the Saigon people faithful to Vien. In the mid-fifties when Vien tried to overthrow the government, he did not need such people as Lautrec, for there was no reason to be secretive. Bao Dai, when he was still emperor, had sold control of the Saigon police to Vien for a million dollars. Vien rapidly turned Saigon into the criminal capital of Indochina. But Vien wasn't satisfied with controlling Saigon; he wanted everything.

"After he fled to Paris, the Binh Xuyen began to fall

apart. Those whose associations with the **Binh Xuyen** were unknown remained in Saigon while the others found refuge in old lairs in the Rung Sat swamps. It did not take those still in Saigon long to discover that they could realize a larger profit if they did not split their net with Vien in Paris or those hiding in the swamps. Soon, Vien found himself receiving little from Saigon. That was when he found Lautrec."

Dupree paused to sip his absinthe and chain-light another Gauloise. Perspiration had begun to form upon his high forehead. He blotted it away with the handker-chief.

"Lautrec," he continued, "quickly made those in Saigon see the error of their ways. You've heard of *Le Butcher?*" I nodded. "That is Lautrec."

Le Butcher. The man responsible for much of the terrorism in the hamlets and outlying villages north of the Mekong Delta, and one of the most wanted men in Southeast Asia. His victims were always hideously muti-lated and found with a poppy flower across their lips.

"Why do the police not arrest him?" I asked.

Dupree smiled, finished his absinthe, and stood. He flicked imaginary dust from his clothes, placed his hat carefully over his forehead, and picked up his cane.

"I should think that would be evident for a man of your intellect," he said. "What did Bay Vien control before he left Vietnam?"

I nodded slowly. "The police. Who's to say who is legitimate?"

"Exactly. Besides, Lautrec's activities have yet to be proven. He is very careful." He turned to depart, but I stopped him.

"How do I get in touch with him?"

"I do not know," he said. He gave me a little smile. "I am a simple broker. Remember? Nothing more."

He bowed his head and touched the brim of his hat in

farewell and left. I sat at the table and went over what he had told me. Point one: Muhl had something working with Lautrec, but what? Point two: Lautrec had a certain amount of protection from the police, but that was not enough because his operation spilled over into military circles as well. Point three: where could I find Lautrec?

I finished my gin and tonic and left the Continental. I had little to go on, but somehow I felt the reason for Muhl's trip to the Michelin Plantation was connected with Lautrec. My reasoning followed no rule of logic, but I knew, with the newsman's sixth sense, that it was true. The three points I had listed meant little without Lautrec. I had to get close to him, and the only person I could think of who might or would help me was Number One Phuong.

I went home to leave a note for Rachel and took a cab to Vo Thanh Street and the 147 Club. The tables and chairs were filled with soldiers, and Dean Martin was again crooning about love from the jukebox. The record sounded worse than before, and I wondered if it was almost worn through. At the table nearest the door an old woman sat with a pack of greasy tarot cards. I asked her if she had seen Number One Phuong. She gestured vaguely towards the rear of the club. I thanked her and moved slowly through the darkness and the accented murmurings of promises and hoarse doubts. A couple of the prostitutes waved vague greetings as I passed, and I returned them, ignoring the soldiers beside them. Most of the soldiers looked as if they would have been more at home in a malt shop than a brothel.

I found Phuong on the lap of a large, black sergeant in the back corner of the club. Phuong had deliberately chosen that spot, I suspected, as the light was the faintest and would help hide the thickening of her features and the tiny lines around the corners of her eyes and lips that

116

defied heavy applications of rice powder. I was saddened by this, as Phuong and I went back a long way. We had even shared a flat above a cafe on what was then Rue Catinet in the early days before her name was Phuong. They had been happy days, and I had even entertained the recklessness of youth and thought about making her my wife, but she was happier doing what she knew best. She was gone when I returned from the Sukarno problem. After a brief reunion, we had parted friends.

The sergeant eyed me carefully when I slid into the chair opposite them, but displayed no animosity.

"Hello, Phuong," I said. She grinned and leaped from his lap and sidled carefully around the table to give me a moist kiss.

"Cheri!" she said and sighed. She appeared to be a little drunk, but I knew it was a pretense, as Phuong would never get drunk until the day's business was over. "I was sorry to hear about your friend."

"Thank you," I said. I looked at the sergeant. "We're just friends. All I want is some information. Okay?"

He shrugged and drank deeply from a half-full bottle of Beer Larue. He placed the bottle on the table and smacked his lips with relish.

"We kind of had an understanding," he said softly, but there was no menace to his words.

"Five minutes," I said. "All I need is five minutes."

"Friends, huh?"

I nodded.

"Private?"

I nodded again.

"What the hell. I have enough time." He slipped gracefully from the table and moved towards the bar.

"Tell Thanh the drinks are on me," I said quickly. He stopped and turned back.

"You don't have to do that."

"I know. It's fair, though."

"Yes," he said and flashed a grin. "It's fair. I'll tell him."

He walked towards the bar, his gait loose-hipped and jaunty, and I made a mental note not to keep Phuong too long: the sergeant was rather big, and the bar bill could be forbidding if I tarried. I turned back to Phuong. She smiled and lifted her glass masquerading as whisky and sipped.

"You are looking well, Phuong," I said. She laughed and replaced her glass upon the table.

"Always I look well, Con," she said. "Unless you look too closely. But there are many soldiers in Saigon these days, and they do not look closely. They are more concerned with how quickly one can leave."

I laughed with her. In the old days, a girl did not hire herself to a bar to cadge drinks from women-hungry G.I.s, but used the bars as meeting places for *union illicite*. Drinking then was minimal, and the man was not looking for a few hours' pleasure, but contemplating a full night's engagement. That was before Madame Nhu's decree that outlawed prostitution and even dancing in Saigon in the fifties. Ostensibly, Madame Nhu's demands to the Assembly were to allow women the social and economic rights they had been denied by mandarin tradition that had relegated women to second-class status since the dynasty founded by Bao Dai's ancestor Gia Long in 1802. But those who knew Madame Nhu were aware of her hedonistic tendencies and suggested she had been jilted by her current lover in favor of a prostitute who later became the mistress of Premier Nguyen Van Tam. Since her husband's assassination, the police had relaxed enforcement of the decree. Copies of a nude painting by a famous Vietnamese artist who claimed the model was Madame Nhu began to circulate. Although

118

the high-breasted figure did seem to resemble Diem's siter-in-law, there was some doubt as to her real identity. Still, the suggestion that the sensuous nude was Madame Nhu was enough to make the painting very popular among the soldiers on the black market. I remembered the original very well: a delicate painting of soft blues and greens.

"Now, Con," she said, wrinkling her nose at me. "You did not come here to renew old times."

"No," I said. "I came to find a man who is very hard to find."

"What man?" she asked in a guarded whisper. Her face was impassive, her eyes veiled.

"Lautrec," I said.

Fear flashed across her face, then disappeared. Twin lines of concern and disapproval etched themselves between her eyes as she leaned across the table. She suddenly looked her age.

"Be very careful," she said quietly. Her eyes flickered uneasily around the room. "This is not the place to speak of him."

"You know him?" I lowered my voice to match hers.

"I am a *putain*," she said. "All of us know of him. He is a bad man, Con, very bad."

"How do you know him?" I asked.

"He takes a third of all here," she said. Her lips began to tremble. "But do not speak any more about this. It is very bad."

"How do I get to see him?"

"Why do you wish to see him?"

I did not answer, and after a minute she slowly nodded.

"Of course. Your friend."

"Will you help me?"

"No," she said.

"Why?"

"I do not wish to see you hurt," she said. "We are friends."

"I can take care of myself," I said a little stiffly.

"You are being very foolish," she flashed. She was becoming angry. "You sound like the young soldiers who try to impress us with their bravery."

"I'm sorry," I murmured, abashed at her analysis. "But it is very important that I speak to this man."

"Why?"

"Because of . . . Muhl," I finished lamely. I still could not call him my friend. He had caused me nothing but anguish since his arrival, yet I was ready to tilt at windmills, to fight dragons, for a man I detested.

"He was this much a friend to you?" she asked.

"No. He was no friend. But he began something I must finish."

"The war," she said bitterly. "It is making foolish men out of the wise."

"I must ask him some questions," I persisted.

"I do not know where he is," she said resignedly. "But I will try to find out for you, and then you can pretend to be a hero. Only do not tell anyone that I sent you to him for when you are killed, such knowledge would give to me *la guele d'un revolver*." I knew what she meant: my death would be awkward for her if certain people thought she was an informant.

"I won't say anything," I promised. I reached across the table and squeezed her hands. "Thank you, Phuong. Thank you very much."

"Go away," she said roughly and jerked her hands from my grip. A hint of tears shone in her eyes. "I liked you better when you wrote the stories and did not try to become one."

I rose and crossed to the bar, where the black sergeant patiently waited.

120

"Thank you," I said and laid a twenty piaster note on the bar to cover his tab.

"Any time," he said and looked curiously from me to Phuong and back.

"Bad news?"

"It could be," I said drily. He waited for me to elaborate, and when I didn't, shrugged his shoulders and moved back towards the table. I hoped he would be good to her: I had caused her enough pain for one day.

17

THE DAY HAD grown hotter when I emerged from the cool interior of the 147 Club. I was in no mood for Le Duc Trinh. Unfortunately, he was waiting for me in the back seat of an air-conditioned black Mercedes parked arrogantly in a no-parking zone at the curb in front of the club. I turned to walk away, but the passenger door opened, and a young, gaunt, unsmiling Vietnamese stepped out and blocked my path.

"Mr. Edwards," Trinh called from the interior of the Mercedes. "I wish to speak with you."

Resignedly, I turned back to the car. The young Vietnamese opened the rear door, and I slid into the coolness beside Trinh. He shut the door behind me and got into the front. I felt as if I had fallen into a cobra's den.

"What do you want?" I asked curtly.

"Do not be impatient," he said. He tapped the driver on the shoulder and ordered him to drive. He leaned back in his seat and looked at me as the Mercedes purred smoothly away from the curb. Traffic halted to let it move into the stream, and then gave it a wide berth.

"You have some very strange friends, Mr. Edwards," he lisped. He gave me a faint smile.

I shrugged and stared at the shops as we passed them. He laughed quietly and clicked his tongue disapprovingly against his teeth.

"You disappoint me, Mr. Edwards. I thought we could be friends."

"Why?" I asked. I turned back to him. His eyes were bright with amusement. "Why should we be friends?"

"Because of our respective jobs. One never knows when such a friend as myself would be helpful."

"What do you want?" I asked again. "I am a very busy man."

"Yes. I know that you are," he said smoothly. "But, as I said, be patient. All in good time, all in good time."

"Where are we going?"

"Do not worry," he said and gave another small laugh. "Really, Mr. Edwards. I believe you have seen too many of your American gangster films."

"The resemblance is uncanny," I said. "Innocent man leaves club and is forced into mysterious black car and is taken for a ride. No questions answered, destination unknown. You're right: it's very clichéd and hackneyed. So why are you doing it?"

He ignored my question, a tactic designed to make someone uneasy, in that it suggested ultimate power over the individual asking the question. It worked. I was extremely uneasy and upset at myself for allowing Trinh to make me feel that way. I tried to tell myself that he was an arrogant man cognizant of his own importance, possessed of a bloated will. But my practicality reminded me that he could afford to be this way because he was omnipotent and misanthropic—two traits deadly to the unwary.

"Have you learned anything from your friends?"

"Such as?"

He gave me a pained expression and tapped me gently upon my knee with a bony finger. I moved my knee away.

"Do not take me for a fool, Mr. Edwards. That would be very dangerous. You know to what I refer."

"You're being very enigmatic," I said.

"And you are stalling. What have you learned?"

I sighed and slumped against the leather cushions of the Mercedes. Obviously, he was going to keep on in this vein until he knew. But I could not tell him about

123

Lautrec. I remembered Dupree's words. Who could I trust?

"Not much," I said. I tried to sound dejected and bitter. "All I know is that he was working on a story. About what and whom, I do not know. No one seems to know. In fact, every time I try to find some hint, some idea, no one will talk to me. What have you discovered?"

I boldly looked at him. He met my eyes in silence for a long moment, then reached forward and tapped the driver on the shoulder. Instantly, the Mercedes swung to the curb and stopped. I looked around with interest. We were in the market area.

"I do not believe you," he said slowly, "but I will give you the benefit of the doubt. I hope you have learned something when next we have a little chat. Do not try to play games with me, Mr. Edwards. You are not equipped for such intrigue."

The young Vietnamese opened the door. I stepped out into the bright sunlight. A sheen of perspiration immediately formed upon my forehead.

"One more thing."

I turned back to the car and leaned down.

"A word of advice. I would not visit the 147 Club for the next few days if I were you. The atmosphere might become very unhealthy. Goodbye, Mr. Edwards."

He nodded at the driver, and the Mercedes moved away from the curb. Again, the traffic parted, and faces turned to curiously regard me. It was unusual for one to be let out of a police car in the market.

I tried to hail a cab, but the drivers passed me without looking. Trishaws, too, ignored me. Puzzled, I turned to a melon stand, but the young girl quickly moved to help another customer. Then it dawned on me, and I swore softly as I realized Trinh had marked me as a friend of the police.

124

I turned and walked rapidly away from the market toward Tu Do Street. Perspiration began to trickle down my sides and back. I knew I would not find a ride for several blocks. It was subtle demonstration from Trinh to remind me of his power and a warning that he expected more cooperation the next time.

18

I DID NOT hear from Phuong for several days. In the meantime, I attended wearisome press conferences, entertained Rachel and some of my colleagues at the Continental, and tried to find leads on Muhl's project. I even tried to bribe the police officer at Muhl's apartment, but he was one of the rare honest breed and threatened to arrest me if I didn't leave. I even enlisted Tran Am to ask his friends if Muhl had contacted them, but Tran Am came up with nothing save a rather large bill for expenses. I paid him for a piece of useful information that made a short, but nice feature on the theft of a penicillin shipment from the Navy Store in Cholon.

My life was threatening to sink back into the daily routine B.M.—Before Muhl (the double-entendre did not escape me)—when Tran Am appeared near noon one day and silently handed me a note. It was from Phuong.

"Con," it read. "Very sick. Please come. Have what you want. Please help. Phuong." Again, twelve words. Was a mischievous god somewhere taunting me with macabre symbolism? I shuddered and looked at Tran Am.

"Can you take me to her?"

He nodded.

"Now."

He nodded again, and I stood and automatically stuck a pad and pen into my pocket and moved towards the door. He stopped me and looked seriously at me.

"It will be dangerous, very dangerous," he said. "Do you not have a pistol?"

126

"No," I said. "It is against the law."

He shook his head and nervously bit his lip. The pistol, I could see, was very important to him. He was reluctant to go unless we were armed.

"Where is she?" I asked.

"Dakow. She is not well. Hurt badly."

"How?" I said. I grabbed his arm and gently shook him. "How is she hurt?"

"Bad mans beat her, cuts her. You no have pistol?"

"No," I said. "Take me to her anyway."

"Must have pistol," he said stubbornly. He pushed my hand from his arm. "You no understand. Very dangerous."

"Would five thousand piasters make it less dangerous?"

He looked into my eyes and saw that I was serious. Confusion crossed his features while he tried to think why I was so insistent on accompanying him without a pistol. Had he not warned me of the danger?

"She mean this much?" he asked.

"She is a friend," I said. "An old friend who needs my help. That is all."

His face cleared, and he vigorously nodded his head. Friendship he understood. It was a quality more rare and valued in Saigon these days than the inflated piaster, and, consequently, made the risk acceptable to Tran Am.

"Come," he said. "I will take you to her."

I locked the door behind us and followed him down the staircase to the street. I raised my arm to call a taxi, but he hastily pulled it down.

"No," he said. "There is another way. Follow me."

He led me rapidly down back streets. I followed him warily, stepping wide of shadows and trying to avoid the garbage carelessly dumped over the streets by scavengers in search of food.

We emerged on the Quay Lemoine, where the shrimp boats arrived. Tran Am moved quickly among the sampans looking for someone. He found him placidly eating a bowl of rice aboard a sampan tucked back in the shadows formed by a concrete retaining wall. A quick argument followed as the man finished his rice and carefully stowed the bowl in a small box. He moved to the stern of the sampan and began to untie the sweep as Tran Am hurried back to collect me.

"He will take us," he said, "But we must hurry. It will cost fifty piasters." He spat into the water and glowered at the boatman. "Someday. Someday he go too far."

"Can you trust him?" I asked. He looked astounded.

"Of course," he said with surprise. "He is my uncle!"

"Good enough," I said and moved towards the sampan.

"You must hide. Beneath the *vai-bo*. Quickly!"

He urgently pushed my head down, and I crawled beneath the canvas stretched over four poles and tried to make myself comfortable among the nets and pots and pans that littered the bottom of the boat. The stench was almost overpowering: melons, mangosteen, guava, paw-paw, moldy vegetables, and, I discovered after removing the cover of an earthen pot, rotting fishheads that, I presumed, the old fisherman planned on using for bait. (I later was told he probably intended to use them for *Wak-To* sauce.) I pulled my handkerchief from my pocket and pressed it to my nose. Tran Am noticed my discomfort and chuckled.

"We will soon be there," he said. "Try not to breathe. Is bad. Very bad. But my uncle, he is worker, and the smell is an honest one." He frowned. "Except now. I do not know why."

"It doesn't matter," I said, my voice muffled through the folds of the handkerchief. "Forget it. A trifle."

"You do not understand," he insisted. "He charge *me!*"

He sounded petulant and angry, but I did not smile. I knew what he meant. The family was the focus of life in

Saigon these days. It did not matter what one did, the family always was a pillar of support. It was a form of life that had been thrust upon them by the mandarin government of Gia Long and reemphasized by the war. The family came first; fortunes second. By demanding money from Tran Am, his uncle had stepped outside the family. I began to worry and wondered if the uncle had suddenly developed northern sympathies.

The prow rasped against a concrete piling on the Cholon side, and Tran Am scampered out to hold the sampan steady as I clumsily climbed over the side and made my way to the top of the quay. He murmured something to his uncle, who shrugged and slipped a rope around the sweep's handle. He squatted on his heels and stared blankly at me. I did not like his stare and briefly wished I'd had a pistol to bring with me.

"Come," Tran Am said, after he joined me on top. He walked rapidly from the quay, glancing left and right at the silent faces that ignored us. I followed him as he turned into a narrow, twisting street filled with people that reminded me of the Chinese section in Singapore: the same crumbling concrete walls, the same cracked and peeling wooden doors, the same smells of hot pepper and a certain cloying sweetness reminiscent of opium, the same impassivity, the same subdued clamor as I passed. It seemed a place ready for the Tong wars, not a place for an overactive imagination.

We wove our way through several streets, twisting back upon our path to see if anyone followed us. I was panting from the heat and exertion when Tran Am darted between two narrow buildings and disappeared through a dingy and dark doorway. I hurried after him and found myself at the foot of a narrow stairway that led upward. We mounted the stairs and paused in front of a door once painted bright red, but now faded to the color of dried blood. Tran Am knocked softly.

"Who is it?" a voice called from within. I was surprised: whoever was behind the door had spoken in English, and, if I did not miss my guess, was American.

"I have brought him," Tran Am said. "Open. We are alone."

"Tell him to speak," the voice demanded.

"Con Edwards," I said. I felt a little self-conscious at the melodrama we were playing, but a cold chill on the back of my neck reminded me of the need for melodramatic precaution. Perhaps it was preconditioning from old Alan Ladd-Audie Murphy films, but the sense of danger was still there despite my desperate wish for cynicism.

"Come in," the voice ordered. "Slow. Very slow."

Tran Am opened the door and motioned me in front of him. I kept my hands half-raised in front of me and stepped inside. There wasn't much light inside the room, but I could make out the shadowy figure in front of me and the U.S. Colt .45 pistol steady in his hand. Tran Am followed me in, and I heard the door click shut behind us.

"Well, I'll be damned," the figure said. "So you're Con Edwards."

"Do I know you?" I asked politely, squinting to make out the figure's features.

"You should," he said and switched on a small lamp upon a table. It was the black sergeant from the 147 Club. My face must have mirrored my surprise, for he chuckled and carefully eased the hammer down on the .45.

"Yes. I can see you remember," he said. "Imagine my surprise when Phuong told me you were the famous Con Edwards. A friend sends me clippings of your stuff from the States. Pretty good. You truthful, man."

"Thank you," I said. "But I don't know your name."

"Jackson. Sergeant Andy Jackson. And the middle name's Jefferson. My old man," he explained with a smile at my surprise, "read a book once on the two and couldn't make up his mind which one he liked the best. I'm with the 173rd Airborne Brigade (Separate)."

"What happened? Where's Phuong?" I asked.

"In there." He gestured with the pistol to a doorway on the right. "She's pretty bad off. They caught us as we was leaving some little bar on the waterfront. 'Bout two days after you left. We'd been partying pretty hard. Don't know how or why we ended up there. Mr. Jackson's boy surely wasn't thinking straight. First thing I know, I'm stretched out in the gutter with a knot on my head, and she's beside me, ripped and bleeding. They carved her up badly," he added, as I moved past him to the doorway and entered the room.

Phuong lay wrapped in bandages on the bed. I would not have known her if she had not opened her eyes and looked at me. It was their expression, accusing, yet warm, that told me who she was.

"Hello, Phuong," I said. A lump formed in my throat as I moved to her side. I gently took her hand. Her fingers pressed against mine in recognition, then relaxed. I turned my head and looked at the sergeant.

"They cut her larynx," he said softly. "Her larynx and her nipples, and slit her nose. I thought she was dead. Took two hundred and seven stitches to close her up."

"How did you get here?" I asked.

"Friend of mine from the hospital runs a little business on the side. He found us this place and got some doctor to treat her."

I looked back at Phuong. She tried to smile through the bandages, but winced in pain and closed her eyes. A tear ran from her eye down her cheek, and I brushed it away.

"I'm sorry, Phuong," I said. Her fingers pressed my hand hesitantly.

"Was it Lautrec?" Her head inclined fractionally. She pulled her hand free and gestured for something upon which to write. I pulled the pad and pen from my pocket and placed them in her hands. Carefully, she laid the pad in her lap and, without looking, traced the message in block letters: WAREHOUSE. QUAI LEMOINE. CAREFUL.

I showed the note to Tran Am. "Do you know it?" I asked.

He nodded. "But it is many buildings. Is there a number?"

I turned back to her and asked, "Phuong?"

Her eyes flickered, and she wrote: SANS VASE-LINE.

I felt a smile tugging at the corners of my mouth. I patted her hand.

"I remember," I said. It was one of the coarse jokes from the dice game of *Quatre Cent Vingt-et-un* that we had played years ago when we were together. It was, in fact, the first roll I had made when I first played with her for drinks at the old Le Ronde. A four-two-one.

"I still believe you cheated," I said. Her eyes crinkled with amusement.

"Can you tell me anything else?" I asked.

Her eyes frowned, and the sergeant spoke. "Take it easy on her. She needs her rest."

She blinked her eyes at him and traced out another note: MUHL LOOK FOR MOLLY.

"Molly? A woman?" Phuong nodded. "Molly. Do you know anyone by that name?"

Her lips pulled down and she scribbled intently for a minute, then handed me the note: WHAT NAME MOLLY? NO PAY SUCH NAME.

I grinned. Phuong was ever the business woman.

"You're sure about the name?"

She pressed my fingers again. I bent and kissed her on the forehead. Her brow was wet and felt feverish to my lips.

"Don't worry about anything," I said. "You'll be safe here."

"She won't worry, man," the sergeant said. "I'll be right here with her."

Phuong gave him a tiny smile and arched her eyebrow at me. I shook my head and patted her hand.

"I'll be careful. You need him here. Now, you get some rest. I'll send a few things over with Ha Bo. Okay?"

She nodded, pressed my hand once more, and closed her eyes. I gently removed my hand and walked back to the small sitting room. Tran Am followed, and we waited as the sergeant carefully tucked the blankets around her and did the minor fussing with the room that people do when they wish there was more they could do.

"Who is this Ha Bo?" Sergeant Jackson asked suspiciously as he joined us. "I don't want any stranger around here. How will I know him?"

Tran Am laughed, and I had to smile. Ha Bo was one of those evolutionary misfits that P. T. Barnum made a fortune from by exposing them to the public years ago as freaks. He would have welcomed Ha Bo with opened arms and an open-end contract. The average Annamese was around five-eight in height and as slender as a reed. Ha Bo was close to seven foot and three hundred pounds, none of it fat. He had been an apprentice to a blacksmith in the north and had left when the Vietminh forces had overrun his village. He worked on the docks and was the only man I knew who could tuck a full cask of palm oil under one arm. He was the strongest man I had ever met, but had the mind of a ten-year-old. Privately, I thought it was a pituitary disorder that had made him so different from the others of his race. He was also gentle, and fiercely loyal, and Phuong's brother. I could think of no one more devoted who could offer her such excellent protection. I explained this to the sergeant.

"Shit," he said. "You ain't described a man, you described a mountain."'

He let us out and firmly locked the door behind us. I

felt drained and much older. I had little energy left, but knew we had to get away from the building. My presence was a danger not only to Phuong, but the sergeant as well.

We retraced our steps to the quay. I was surprised at how long we had been in the tiny apartment. The streets were deserted as the people moved inside to escape the heat of mid-afternoon. My apprehension increased: at least, in a crowd we were much less obvious. Tran Am must have felt the same way, as he increased his speed through the streets.

I have often read how people's fears are magnified and the worst realized at the most inopportune moment. So it was with us when we arrived at the quay where we had left Tran Am's uncle. The sampan was gone.

19

"THIS IS VERY bad," Tran Am said anxiously. His voice had risen slightly with his concern. He looked up and down the quay: it was deserted. We were alone.

"What do we do now?" I asked. My throat was dry, and perspiration was threatening to drip into my eyes.

He shrugged. "There is only the bridge. I do not know any of the boat people here, and it would be very dangerous to ask someone we do not know to take us across."

"How far is the bridge?"

"Not far." He hesitated.

"What is it?" I asked.

"I do not wish to use the bridge," he said simply.

"What is wrong with the bridge?" I asked impatiently. I wanted to move away from the quay, and if the bridge was our only choice, then it made little sense to delay.

"There is nothing wrong with the bridge. It is the problem of getting to the bridge," he explained. "We must go through the Cam Do district to get to the bridge. Do you understand?"

I understood. The Cam Do district had many opium dens and gambling halls that still operated behind closed doors despite the many attempts of the Saigon government over the years to close them down. It was also one of the old Binh Xuyen strongholds during the fifties.

"Do we have another way?" I asked.

"No." He sighed and turned to lead the way from the quay. "But I do not like it. Maybe, maybe we will get lucky and find a police patrol and follow them across the bridge."

We did not get lucky. Three blocks from the bridge, eight Vietnamese surrounded us. It was accomplished quickly and efficiently. Two stepped from a shadowed doorway and blocked our path, while the other six moved in from the sides and back. Tran Am protested angrily, but one of them moved a package he was carrying against his ribs, and Tran Am's face turned a pasty white. We went with them without further argument. They worked casually, but alertly, and forced us down an alley that opened onto a cul-de-sac. Lautrec, dressed in wilted white with a red poppy pinned to his lapel, waited for us at the far end. His thin face broke into a grin at our approach.

"Welcome," he beamed. "I have been waiting to meet you, Mr. Edwards."

"Why?" I asked. My legs began to tremble, and I tightened my muscles in a futile attempt to stop them.

"Because you have been so curious to meet me," he replied. "And we had a friend in common. Poor Mr. Muhl." He shook his head in mock sorrow. "He should not have tried to get involved."

"In what?" I asked. His face showed his surprise.

"You do not know?"

"No. He did not confide in me."

"But are you not in charge?"

"Yes, but he did not tell me what he was working on."

"I see," he said slowly. He thought for a minute. A fly buzzed around my head, but I did not dare swat at it with those eight silent Vietnamese watching. I did not think they would look favorably upon any sudden movement.

"And now you wish to know what he was doing?" I nodded. "Why?"

"I suppose you could call it professional curiosity," I said.

136

"That is unfortunate, this curiosity of yours. I assume you know the old proverb about the cat?"

The grin had slipped from his face, and his black eyes glittered coldly.

"Yes," I said. I ran my tongue around my lips to moisten them. "Yes, I know it. It is the curse of the newsman."

"That is too bad," he said regretfully. "I do not suppose you would give me your word to try and stop this curiosity of yours?"

"Would you believe me if I did?"

"No."

"I did not think so, either."

"But then, you understand, I cannot allow this curiosity of yours to continue."

A cold rivulet of perspiration trickled down my spine. I tried for nonchalance when I answered him, but my voice sounded thick, as if I had drunk too many gin and tonics.

"I understand. So now what? Do you kill me like you did Muhl?"

He laughed. "No, that would not do. Two dead newsmen from the same paper would provide too much coincidence."

"So what do you plan?"

"You have many friends," he said. His eyes slid to Tran Am. He nodded, and before I could protest, one of the Vietnamese stepped forward, placed a pistol against his temple, and pulled the trigger. The sound of the shot reverberated thunderously in the closed space. Tran Am's head jerked from the impact of the bullet, and he fell to the pavement. His legs twitched spasmodically, then stilled. For a strange reason, Long's assassination of the Vietcong terrorist flashed in my mind. *Déjà vu*, I thought and turned back to Lautrec. His lips smiled thinly at me.

"Now you have one less."

"You son of a bitch. Why?" I felt as if I was going to vomit. The smell of Tran Am's blood clogged my nostrils. I swallowed heavily and gasped for air. Heavy bluebottles already buzzed in eager anticipation.

"It is a warning what will happen to the rest of your friends," he said. "If you persist, you will be their executioner." He stared down at Tran Am for a moment, then raised his eyes to meet mine.

"Make no mistake, Mr. Edwards," he said harshly. "This will happen again. Do not think of vengeance. Think only of your own stupidity, for that is what caused this. Now go. There is nothing more you can say or do here. My men will see you safely across the bridge."

He unpinned the poppy from his lapel and bent down and laid it carefully over Tran Am's lips. I felt a nudge in my back and turned to go. Lautrec's voice stopped me.

"Incidentally, Mr. Edwards," he called softly. "It was not I who killed your friend Muhl."

He nodded at the Vietnamese, and I was gently pushed forward. I stumbled down the alley, my mind racing with what I had been told. I did not doubt his word. He had no reason to lie. He had deliberately killed Tran Am not only as a warning, but as a demonstration as well that he did not fear having anyone know him as a murderer. I felt helpless and enraged. Tran Am had died for nothing. I was also deeply afraid.

20

Rachel was reading Zola's *Nana* in the wicker chair in front of the wide-open French windows when I arrived home. There was a tall cold drink sitting on the bamboo table beside her. Her honey-colored legs were hooked over the back of a chair. Her blouse was unbuttoned to catch whatever breeze might blow in from the street, but the leaves of the tamarind trees were still, and the mahogany blades of the ceiling fan were churning mightily against the muggy air. Perspiration was pouring off me, and I was still shaking. I headed directly to the liquor cabinet and poured a full glass of rum. It didn't help, and I poured another. Rachel watched with that short-tempered amusement that is really sarcasm and disgust.

"Let me guess," she said acidly. "You've either been fired or left off the press junket to Nha Trang."

"Wrong on both counts," I said. I drained the glass, shuddered, and felt a little better. I poured another drink.

"Then you just had a sudden urge to commit suicide through cirrhosis of the liver," she said. "Couldn't you at least say 'hello' before beginning to self-destruct?"

"Hello," I said. I took another swallow. I thought: this whole situation is insane! Tran Am has just been brutally murdered, and you're mouthing inanities from some Noel Coward drawing-room comedy. All we need is Jeeves walking in with a silver salver of cucumber sandwiches.

"How quaint," she began, but I interrupted.

"Tran Am is dead. Murdered."

Her eyes flickered in confusion for a moment, then the skin around her cheekbones tightened, and her heels slipped off the chair with a crash as she jerked upright in the chair.

"My God!" she said. "How?"

"Lautrec," I answered. My hands began to shake. "He shot him just as Loan did that Vietcong. Single bullet through the temple. I saw it." I drained my glass.

"Why?" She tossed Zola on the floor and picked up her glass.

"As a warning. Muhl's death is a closed book. Chapter one has been written, and there is to be no chapter two."

"You went to the police, of course."

"No."

"For heaven's sake, why not?" she asked angrily. "The man committed murder!"

"Because I have a lot of friends. Such as you," I said wearily. I picked up the rum bottle and crossed to the armchair and sank heavily into it.

"Besides, which police do I go to? Who?

She gave me a puzzled look and said, "I don't understand. Why can't you go to the police?"

I almost smiled. Her midwestern naiveté was showing. The police were all paragons of virtue, their hands unsullied by Evil, the saviors of Arthur, the Guardians of the Grail. It was not her fault; she was the product of a teaching system that ignored reality and founded its curriculum upon John Wayne. Which isn't all bad; the problem is knowing when to leave dreams to the aesthetes and move directly to brutal reality.

"I don't know which of the police I can trust," I said, and patiently gave her a capsule lecture on the Binh Xuyen, Bao Dai, the Hoa Haos, and Cao Dais. I explained the various manipulations of power and how Diem had tried to exorcise Bay Vien and Ba Cut from the government by defeating Bay Vien's Binh Xuyen in a bloody street battle that ended with the kingpin of vice fleeing to Paris, and the arrest and subsequent guillotining of Ba Cut. But I reminded her that he did not arrest crime. Rather, Diem had forced it underground as in the case of the Cosa Nostra-Mafia-Lucky Luciano cases in the twenties, thirties, forties, fifties, and, for all I knew, sixties, in the United States.

"Criminals," I said, "often emerge as national heroes. Take General Trinh Minh The of the Cao Dais, who ended up a fierce supporter of the government after receiving more than a million dollars 'incentive money' to forget his alliance with the Binh Xuyen and Hoa Hao. General The also took control of the Saigon government during the transition period immediately following Diem's assasination. Criminals are always there. God may have banished the snake from the Garden of Eden, but Satan was still there in the minds and desires of Adam and Eve. That is the strength of crime: the desires of the people who have a taste for the forbidden. And in places like Saigon where you find hypocrites like Madame Nhu and General The, you will find a willing market. War increases the taste for the forbidden because it increases the fanatic desire to experience all of life, for tomorrow you may die, thank you Omar Khayyám."

I paused to pour another rum, then plunged again into my story. The afternoon deepened as I left my narrative and began to speculate wildly on the recent happenings. Rachel listened patiently, rising only to pour herself a drink now and then, silently letting me purge myself of the terrible fear that threatened to make me vomit despite the doses of rum I swallowed. Finally, I began to run down, the fear being replaced by a feeling of foolishness. Men fall apart in helpless tears or drunken incapacities where women carry on. I have a theory this is a genetic evolution from endless years of burying sons and husbands from the first Cro-Magnon battle through Babylon to date. There can be no other explanation.

Rachel silently watched me. At least, I think she watched me. Her eyes had that faraway look of a Hindu swami in a trance. Involuntarily, I looked over at the carved ivory Buddah sitting on my desk. He wore a satisfied half-smile as if he had just had a successful bowel movement. I wondered if there was a connection between him and womanhood when confronted with the weaknesses of man.

"I see," she said slowly. "You were protecting me. That's why you didn't go to the police."

"Congratulations," I said. "You figured it out."

"Shut up," she said. She looked at me pityingly. "The truth of the matter is you didn't go to the police because you were afraid. You're still afraid, aren't you? You're afraid of Trinh, you're afraid of Lautrec, you're afraid of getting involved. In fact, I think you are truly looking for a way to get rid of the obligation you feel towards Muhl. You really didn't want Tremayne's old job, did you? You just didn't want Muhl to have it. You are quite content to stay quietly in the background, away from the *Times,* writing your safe little pieces, not making decisions. Well, I've got news for you: you are involved whether you like it or not."

She was right: I was afraid, and no man likes to have his fears pointed out to him. It is a sort of mental castration that takes his manhood away from him as certainly as a surgeon's scapel makes an eunuch. Lautrec had done that to me by killing Tran Am, but in doing so, he had left me with little choice: I could not stop now. It was like one of those inane challenges thrown in a child's face by the playground bully. One had to fight or remember the ridicule for the rest of his life. Stupid and senseless though it was, I had no choice: what Muhl had begun, I had to finish, for now I was involved.

"You're right," I said heavily. "Damn it, you're right."

Her features softened, and she rose, crossed to me, and sat in my lap. Her eyes glistened with pride or tears. I could not tell, perhaps both. She gave me a kiss and laid her head upon my shoulder.

"What are you going to do?" she asked softly.

"I think," I said slowly, "I had better see your Colonel Black."

I placed my arms around her and held her tightly as shadows lengthened in the room.

21

COLONEL BLACK SAT unmoving in Muhl's chair in the *Times* office. His eyes turned inward as he carefully reviewed what I had just told him: the peculiarities of Muhl's death, my converstaions with Dupree and Le Duc Trinh, Phuong's mutilation, and my confrontation with Lautrec and Tran Am's death. Perspiration ran down his face and wilted his khaki collar. It was hot and humid in the office, made that way by the virga outside, a condition in which the air was so saturated with moisture it should have been raining, but was not.

At last he sighed and pulled a handkerchief from a back pocket to mop his face.

"So." He looked at me keenly. His eyes were sharp and piercing and set deep in the fleshy folds of his face.

"So. What do you want me to do?"

"I don't know," I said in surprise. "I thought you could give me some answers."

"On what? A conspiracy? You really do not have much of anything, just some wild speculations. The only true connection you have is the death of Muhl, which you claim was murder, and the death of Tran Am, which you know is murder. But you cannot prove either of the two was murder."

"I saw . . . ," I began, but he waved off my protest.

"What you saw is immaterial. By your own admission there were six others there at the time." He shook his head in disgust. "Why do you think Lautrec had them there? That precise number?" I shrugged. "Alibi. They

144

could swear he had nothing to do with Tran Am's death. They could even accuse you of killing him."

"What about Phuong?"

"A whore is always beaten up. That's one of the risks of the trade. Forget about Muhl," he added, anticipating my next comment. "Those wounds could have been caused by anything."

"And what about Lautrec's association with the Binh Xuyen?" I asked, smarting under his dissection.

"That, now," he said softly, "is a different story. We'd love to catch him, but even then we'd have to be careful because we only have circumstantial evidence, and," he smiled wryly, "he would have to be tried in the Vietnamese courts. You already know what that would bring. You were right with your guess about the Binh Xuyen and the Saigon government. We've suspected members of the Binh Xuyen for a long time, but again, there's the matter of proof."

"So I have nothing," I said bitterly. "Two men are dead, and my friends threatened, and there's absolutely nothing I can do."

"No," he said, staring at me thoughtfully. "There is one thing you can do."

"And that is?"

"Keep looking. Find out what Muhl was working on. That's your link: Muhl's story. Maybe you'll come up with some answers that will give us the questions we need."

"But what about Rachel and my other friends? Lautrec meant what he said."

"I'm sure he did," Colonel Black said calmly. "You'll just have to work fast enough to get the answers before Lautrec decides who is going to be the next example."

"But where do I start?" I asked. "I can't go back to Lautrec, and my street credibility is pretty well destroyed after that last trick by Le Duc Trinh."

"Why don't you try that friend of yours, Dupree? Maybe he could give you some answers."

"He's a policeman," I said tiredly.

"No," Colonel Black said, "He's not a policeman. But who else could Muhl have known? He wasn't here long enough to build up many contacts. Why don't you try becoming Muhl?"

"That thought," I said, "is highly repugnant."

He shrugged. "What else do you have? You have to begin at the beginning. Right now, you only have conclusions you've drawn in the dark."

He picked up his battered briefcase and rose. "Keep me informed. I wish you luck." He turned to go and paused by the door. "But don't waste any time."

"One last thing," I ventured.

"Yes?"

"Do you know a woman named or calling herself 'Molly'?"

He pursed his lips and stared thoughtfully into space for a moment, then shook his head.

"No. Why? Is she important?"

"Could be," I said. "Muhl knew her. Or, at least, was looking for her."

"You think she might know something?"

"I don't know. Can you check?"

"I'll run her name through the computers. Meanwhile, watch yourself." He opened the door and closed it behind him. I could hear his heavy tread going down the stairs.

I thought about what he said before he left. I had no intentions of becoming Muhl, but one thing Colonel Black said gave me an idea. Muhl had not been here long enough to build up many contacts. The Vietnamese were very suspicious of foreigners after many bad experiences in the past with misplaced trust. The contacts Muhl had among them I had given him. The only contacts he could

146

have developed on his own would have to have been made among those with whom he had a common ground. I had been looking in the wrong place: I should have begun where he would have had to begin and not where he ended. I should have started looking for the answers with MAC-V and the American forces.

But where to begin?

I leaned back in my chair and let my mind go blank as I stared around the office. The answer, I felt, was not in the bars, or with Lautrec, but here. It had to be. But where? I dismissed the files, for he would not have been so careless as to have kept notes in them after I had refused him permission to work on features. And, why, I asked myself, did it have to get its start as a feature? Why couldn't Muhl have stumbled across something while running the daily routine?

I swung around in my chair and removed the large clipboard filled with the daily assignments from its hook on the wall. Slowly, I thumbed through the massive sheaf of pages, working my way back to the day I left for Plei Me. I began there, discarding his assignments on the daily briefings and press conferences, for I did not think he would have picked up anything at them the other news services would not have received. I was looking for something where Muhl would have had almost exclusive coverage, something so mundane the other services would not have bothered to staff. There was very little, for I had not given him very much following his affair with Rachel.

It took almost three hours, but I finally found it. Two weeks before I left for Plei Me, on November 27, I had assigned Muhl to a story involving the new PX warehouses that had been consolidated under one command. It meant nothing in the way of war coverage, and I remembered trimming the two pages of copy Muhl had submitted upon his return from interviewing the captain and sergeant in charge to four paragraphs and appending them as a filler to the daily log. It wasn't much, but it was the only thing I could find that was not staffed by any other news service and would have brought him into contact with someone I did not know.

I rose and crossed to the filing cabinets and searched for Muhl's original story. I found it and pulled it out and read it. I could see nothing in it that suggested anything further, just an overlong and expanded story about how field PXs could be more efficiently supplied due to the consolidation that provided a central shipping point instead of the four different ones used before. Under the new consolidation, our boys would be able to purchase cameras, radios, chewing gum, cigarettes, nylons, anything to make their lives in the field more bearable. Not much, as I said before, but I had to start somewhere. I made a note of the captain and the sergeant and left for the Central Exchange to visit with them.

22

"I'M NOT QUITE sure I know what you're after, Mr. Edwards," Captain Abraham Lenwald said. He handed my press credentials back to me and led the way into his office. The air-conditioner whirred smoothly in one corner and made the office a place of refuge from the hot warehouse outside. The floor was carpeted, the walls a clean white and unadorned save for a neat bulletin board on one and a framed photograph of Lyndon Johnson on another. Lenwald moved behind the desk flanked on either side by gray filing cabinets and sat. He motioned me to a chair opposite him.

"We're really not news here, although we do serve a viable and important function. Can you give me some idea how I can help you?" he said apologetically.

He was young, filled with that eagerness of youth to succeed in a job that carried no glamour, no military strategic purpose, and no chance of medals except the Army Commendation Medal. It was a job that would not bring him to the attention of his commanding officer and the promotion board unless he made a monstrous mistake, and that he could not afford. He was in a form of purgatory, whether by accident or not, and could only work hard and thankless hours to escape it.

"I would be happy to enlighten you," I said and slipped into the old fallback of the newsman on a follow-up story. "We would like to see just how effective this consolidation has proven, what adjustments have been made, sort of a feature on how the army is always looking for ways of cutting deadwood and saving tax dollars by combining programs and finding the right person to make it work."

It was a poor excuse and would have made a story any self-respecting wire editor would have consigned to the wastebasket, but an officer's career is made in a war zone, and the captain in his eagerness to bring his position to the attention of his superiors, could only see his name in print and the public awareness of himself if such an article was printed. He leaped at the chance and gave me carefully documented charts and figures he had prepared that showed the flow of commercial items to the field before the consolidation and after. The speed with which the items were dispatched showed an average of three days sooner since the consolidation and made for an increased volume of commodities, most notably cameras, radios, cigarettes, and alcoholic beverages.

"PX sales have climbed an average of twenty-nine and one-half percent since the consolidation," he said smugly. "We have increased our orders to thirty-five percent as a result of this, and gross receipts are up thirty-three percent. Although it is becoming harder to satisfy the demand, and we may have to go to forty percent before Christmas, I think we have most definitely shown the consolidation was well worth the effort."

"How many orders are processed each day?" I asked out of politeness.

"About two hundred," he said proudly. "Before the consolidation, about eighty because we had to contact each warehouse for different items that may have been on the list."

"How about loss and breakage?" I asked.

"Halved," he said promptly and showed me another chart to prove his point. "As you can see, with decreased need for handling, the loss potential has dropped significantly in the case of all resalable items. No, Mr. Edwards, this consolidation works."

I murmured my admiration for his administration, promised him a copy of the story when it was written, and took my leave. On my way out of the warehouse, I stopped off to see Sergeant Larry Bowman, a tall, hatchet-faced, laconic Tennessean who was the dispatcher and cargomaster and the other name in Muhl's story. He confirmed Captain Lenwald's story and reiterated the figures on losses and breakage.

"We use ter git 'bout ten to twenty percent cuts on all shipments," he said, "but that's gone now. Ain't nothing move otta here but has mine *and* the captain's signature on it. That's *all* shipments without exception. One of us meets every shipment at the docks, supervises its unloading and brings it directly here. All manifests check off the ships to the docks and off the trucks to here. This is one efficient organization, I tell you." He shifted a plug of tobacco in his cheek and accurately spat a long, brown stream into a cuspidor by his desk.

"Fact is," he continued, "wouldn't surprise me none if the brass don't use this as a model for other supply reorganizations. Sure cut costs."

He left to check a truck loaded and ready to leave. I watched as he told the impatient driver to shut off his engine while he checked the contents against the manifest okayed by the captain. The captain climbed disgustedly from the truck and walked outside to have a cigarette while the sergeant began his meticulous check. I strolled after the private and caught up with him just outside the door, where he squatted on his heels and puffed on his cigarette.

"Looks like a hot day," I ventured.

"Don't it, though," he said. He gave me a quick look, then returned his attention to his cigarette.

"Been making many of these runs?" I asked.

"A few," he said. He spat disgustedly into the street. "Used to have a bit of fun between the loadings, but now we have to wait for the load inspection and keep with our trucks because there's no telling when they'll be done and log you out."

"What do you mean?" I asked.

"Used to be they'd take your truck in at, say 0800 hours and tell you to pick it up at, say 1200 hours. The rest of the time was yours," he explained. "Now, they take your truck in and stamp the log with time of departure, and a driver has to turn in the log at the other end and account for any delay in time of departure and arrival. Takes all the fun out of it."

"That's the army for you," I said.

"Yeah. Ain't nothing any more but the old hurry up and wait."

"What happens on the other end after you log in?" I asked.

"Nothing. That's the worst of it. Used to be the EM and officers' clubs would send their own trucks in to the booze warehouse, but now, with this consolidation, only one man is needed because there's only one run. Me. For both the PX and the clubs. Instead of one off-loading, I got three."

I thanked him for his information and left. As far as I could see, I had wasted an afternoon. I was tired, hot, and thirsty, and no closer to finding out what Muhl had been working on. I decided to stop at the Continental for a drink before returning home.

23

I WAS ON my second gin and tonic and feeling much better about the day's events when Dupree showed up. He noticed me at my table on the Continental terrace and walked over.

"May I join you?" he asked. He smiled politely, and I nodded at the chair opposite and motioned for the waiter.

"Pernod," Dupree said to the waiter and carefully hitched up the legs of his white trousers before sitting. He brushed an imaginary fleck of dust from the table before carefully placing his white planter's hat upon it.

"How have you been?" he asked.

"Fine," I said and took a long sip from my glass. The waiter silently placed the Pernod in front of Dupree and left. I lowered my glass and set it back in the saucer.

"I understand you found Lautrec. Pity about Tran Am," he said and took a tiny sip of the Pernod.

I stared at him for a moment, then asked, "Why is it I always seem to find you after one tragedy or the other?"

He shrugged and gave me a half-smile. "I do not know. Fate, perhaps."

"I wonder," I replied.

"Did you find what you were looking for?"

"No," I said shortly. I drank again.

"Perhaps it would be better if you did not look any more," he suggested.

"What do you mean?"

"You apparently are causing someone a great deal of discomfort. First, Phuong, then Tran Am. This obsession of yours is proving very harmful to your friends. I told you to be careful. You are playing in a game with very high stakes. I do not think you should play anymore."

"Is that a warning, Dupree?" I asked.

"Advice, my friend," he said. He smiled again. "I do not want to follow Tran Am."

"Why did you tell me about Lautrec if you did not want me to find him?''

His eyes flickered for a moment, then returned to meet my stare.

"Because we are friends, and I thought the information might deter you." He lifted the Pernod to his lips.

"Did you give Muhl the same advice?" I asked casually.

His hand froze, and he carefully replaced the glass and looked around. He leaned across the table.

"Who told you that?" he asked anxiously.

"You did. Just now," I replied. He sighed and leaned back in his chair. He took a handkerchief from an inside pocket, carefully blotted his hands, and returned it. I caught a faint scent of lilacs.

"So. How did you know?"

"Simple. Muhl did not know that many people. But he did know you. Not very many people in Saigon who know about Lautrec would talk to Muhl. Why did you?"

"It was just harmless chatter," he said. "More information about what had happened in the fifties. He was young and only knew what he had read. It is not the same as hearing about it from one who experienced it."

"Just background information, is that it?"

"He was a reporter. Is it not necessary for a reporter to know all about his subject? Why should I not have told him? I did not know why he was asking."

I leaned back in my chair and stared thoughtfully at him. A vague idea began to gnaw at my mind, but there were too many possibilities to allow it full germination. I only had one fact, and that was how Muhl had come to

154

learn about Lautrec. But I did not know if he had obtained the information, as Dupree said, in idle conversation and then began to work on his story, or if he already had the story and was searching for supportive information when he visited with Dupree. It would have helped if I had known what he was working on, but I did not.

"When did you tell him about Lautrec?" I asked.

He shook his head in doubt and said, "Two, maybe three weeks before he was killed."

I did some rapid calculation. That would make it either the last week in November or the first week in December.

"You're sure?" I asked. "You're absolutely sure?"

He smiled and shook his head condescendingly at me. "Who remembers the dates of such matters? Perhaps it was four or five or even six weeks. It was just idle conversation over a drink. Like now. An accidental meeting, a polite drink together, nothing more."

"Where did you have this drink?"

His brow furrowed in thought. "Here, I believe. It was either here or the Caravelle. I seldom go any other place. Does it matter?"

"No," I said. "Maybe. I don't know."

"I am sorry," he said. He finished his Pernod and stood. He picked up his hat and carefully placed it on his head to avoid mussing his hair. "Now I must go."

"Dupree," I said, "how did you find out about Tran Am?"

"The workers in my warehouse," he said. "The natives know everything about the streets."

"Where is your warehouse?"

"On the Quay Lemoine." He looked at me quizzically. "But I thought you knew that."

"It must have slipped my mind," I said. "By the way, do you know anyone named Molly?"

Something flickered in his eyes, but I could not tell

155

what, as the polite mask slipped quickly back over his face.

"No. Is she American?"

"I don't know. Could be. Has she been at any of the receptions you've attended?"

He shook his head. "I don't think so. Would you like me to check for you?"

"If it wouldn't be too much trouble," I said. "But be careful."

"Do not worry," he said solemnly. "As long as you persist in this business, I shall." He touched the brim of his hat in farewell and left.

I watched him move across the square, a slim, elegant figure of colonial France, and wondered again why he had stayed in Vietnam after the majority of his country-men had left. Perhaps it was the magic of the country and its people, but I did not think so. Somehow, I could not picture him anywhere else but in Vietnam, just as I couldn't see myself back in the States. Both of us had been away so long our roots had been transplanted into different soil. Yet, there was still a strange loyalty to our mother countries. He would always be French just as I would always be American. A strange paradox, for we could never belong totally to one country without the other. Perhaps we were the vanguard of the future world citizen.

I sighed and finished my drink and rose to leave. I was, I thought, becoming too philosophical. I needed to direct my thoughts more to the question at hand. Somehow, I knew Dupree was involved in the total picture, but how, I was not sure. He seemed to be one of those figures an artist needed in the background to complete a painting, but did not know where to place for the most emphasis.

I needed, I decided, to see Phuong again. I hailed a taxi and directed him across the bridge through the Cam Do district and had him drop me in the middle of the shops near the apartment. I did not worry about Lautrec for I knew he meant what he said: I was more valuable alive than dead to him at the moment, but I did not delude myself into thinking that gave me permanent amnesty. He would kill me as a last resort, but only after he realized his threat was not working. In the meantime, I had to keep Lautrec's thugs as far away from my friends as possible.

I worked my way through the narrow streets, pausing at one shop after another. I kept a close watch behind me to see if I was being followed, but saw no one. Still, I felt uneasy and stopped to eat a bowl of noodles from a sidewalk vendor. I drank a cup of tea from another and bought a carved ivory bracelet from an old man etching a plate with acid. I still could not shake the feeling that I was being followed.

I began to move faster and suddenly reversed my steps, ran half a block, and dodged into a laundry. I moved quickly past the startled proprietor, through the beaded curtain at the back of the shop, and emerged into a small courtyard filled with cauldrons of steaming water. Carefully, I picked my way over the slippery cobblestones and ran down a narrow alley. I paused when I exited, got my bearings, and turned, walking briskly in the direction of the river. At the corner of the block, I turned away from the river and began to thread my way through the narrow streets to Phuong's sanctuary. I did not pause when I reached the peeling facade of her building, but ducked into the doorway and ran up the stairs. Furtively, I knocked on the door.

"*Ai do?*" a voice called softly from within.

"Con Edwards," I said. The bolt rattled, and the door opened a crack. I had to look up to meet the stare of the Vietnamese on the other side.

"Ha Bo," I said. "Do you remember me?"

He opened the door just enough to let me slip through.

157

The first thing I saw was the enormous bore of the sergeant's .45 aimed at my forehead. Behind me, I heard Ha Bo shut and lock the door.

"We weren't expecting you," the sergeant said, as he lowered the .45. He eased the hammer down and slipped the pistol into the waistband of his trousers. "Were you followed?"

"I don't know," I said. "I don't think so."

"Sorry to hear about your friend," he said and moved towards the table in the center of the room. "Tea?"

I shook my head and turned to face Ha Bo. His face was impassive, the forehead high and jutting with heavy bone carapaces over his eyes making him appear simian. His nose was flat, and his jaw long and pointed. He seemed to have no neck, his shoulders were heavy with muscle, and his arms were the size of my legs. I have seen smaller sumo wrestlers, none bigger.

"I am sorry, Ha Bo," I said slowly. "I did not mean for your sister to get hurt."

"She hurt bad," he said solemnly.

"Yes," I answered.

"Who hurt Minh?" He used Phuong's real name, for he never understood why she called herself Phuong.

"A very bad man," I answered.

"Who?" he insisted, and he raised one hand in a fist.

"We haven't told him," Sergeant Jackson said from behind me. "He asks us all the time, but his sister says not to tell him, so I don't."

"Con, you friend. You tell Ha Bo," the gentle giant pleaded.

I shook my head. "Sorry, Ha Bo," I said gently. "I can't. Not yet." His face fell in disappointment. "But would you watch the stairs? Some bad men may have followed me here. Do not let them come in, but do not let them see you either."

His eyes brightened, and he looked at me closely. "These bad men same same bad things Minh?"

158

"Yes," I said. "Same bad men."

"I watch. Hope come," he said and opened the door. He paused, turned, and looked at me. I could almost see his mind working. "You lock." He closed the door softly behind him. I locked the door and turned back to the sergeant.

"How are things?" I asked.

He sighed and sipped from a cup of tea. His eyes were tired and hooded, and the lines around the corners of his mouth had deepened. His beard showed silver against the mahogany of his cheeks. I wondered how much of the silver I had put there.

"He's not very smart," he said, "but I'm glad he's here."

"He has the mind of a ten-year-old," I said, "but how many ten-year-old Vietnamese children do you know who can make themselves understood in English?"

"Not many," he confessed. "In fact, when you put it that way, he's not dumb at all."

"Never make that mistake," I cautioned. "There's a world of difference between ten-year-old Americans and ten-year-old Vietnamese. How many ten-year-olds do you know who have been forced to kill to survive?"

"That's not what I meant," he said. He rubbed his hands over his eyes. "Christ, I don't even know what I meant. I'm too damn tired."

I felt sorry for him. His leave had turned into a nightmare. He might as well have been back on patrol in the jungle for all the rest he had had, but beneath the pity, I felt admiration. Not many men would have done what he was doing. Most soldiers would have left Phuong lying in the street and not assumed responsibility. That showed the compassion of Sergeant Jackson. I liked him.

"I understand," I said. "Have you had any problems?"

"No," he said. "And I'm as jumpy as if I was the sole nigger at a Ku Klux Klan rally." He gave a short laugh

159

and looked up at me. "I don't know much about what's going on, but I can tell you it ain't right."

"I'm afraid I don't understand," I said.

He gestured impatiently. "If the enemy hits you as hard as they hit us the other night, then doesn't return to finish the job, something's screwy. Look," he explained at my confusion. "In the jungle, the enemy first makes a probing attack to find your strengths and weaknesses, then falls back and hits you with everything they've got. Understand?" I nodded. "Well, they never returned. Nothing. And they had us."

"This isn't the jungle," I said.

"Isn't it?" He scrubbed his hands over his face and gave me a pitying look. "Don't kid yourself. These dudes are bad. They wouldn't have done that to her if they were just trying to scare us. Something's happened, and I don't know what. Either they have found bigger game somewhere else, or we were nothing but a decoy, or . . . ," he hesitated and shook his head.

"Or," I prompted.

"Reinforcements have arrived, and although I think that mountain out there is a threat, he can't fight bullets. Is there something, someone, giving us a hand?"

"Maybe you're reading too much into this," I said soothingly. "Maybe this was a warning to me."

"No," he said firmly. "I don't know what you're involved in, but if they killed that friend of yours, Tran Am, then they should have killed her. And me. It makes more sense. Why do both? Cripple her and kill him? They could have killed her, and that would have accomplished the same thing. It doesn't make sense. The only thing I can think of is someone is dealing himself into this game. Who?"

"I don't know," I said. "You're right, though: it doesn't make sense. Phuong's death would have had the same significance as Tran Am's and there would have been less risk."

160

"There you go," he said. "Now, I think that maybe you'd better tell old Andy Jackson just what's going down."

"Well," I said and pulled a chair out from the table and sat. "It's a long story."

Briefly, I told him about Muhl and the Binh Xuyen. I explained about Lautrec and Le Duc Trinh and my visit to Central Supply. I omitted nothing: he had earned the entire story. After I finished, he nodded thoughtfully, then rose and walked to a cupboard and removed a bottle of Scotch. He poured each of us a glass, then placed the bottle between us, and returned to his seat.

"Sounds like a clicker in the woodpile to me," he said. He chuckled at my expression and explained. "During the depression, the Ku Klux Klanners used to wait until the Negroes had cut their wood for winter, then tried to steal it. The expression means using somebody's work for your own benefit."

"You know," I said slowly so as not to give offense, "your erudition surprises me."

He grinned. "Tuskegee Institute, 1952. Not soon enough to mean anything in a white man's world, but too late to mean the back of the bus. They made me a sergeant. Sergeant-major, that is, E-9, one step below an officer. I'm the original token."

"You seem to take it very well," I said. "You would be at least a major if you were white."

"What the hell," he said. "If I was just a few years younger, it might have made a difference. But now, I'm close to retirement, and those who upset the applecart reap only spoiled apples. It doesn't matter. I have no one but myself and a little place on Matecumbe Key, paid for, where I'll retire in four years."

"I hope you make it," I said.

The grin slipped a bit from his face. "Me, too."

"Tell me again how you found this place. That seems a little strange."

"I called a friend at Ton Son Nuht who has been doing a little dealing on the side," he explained. "Just a little dope, you understand, the soft stuff like diet pills, grass, nothing heavy. I guess 'friend' is a bit much, more like an 'acquaintance' I've suspected," he added. "He arranged for a doctor to attend Phuong and found us this place."

"But how did he find this place?" I persisted. "This is not exactly the Continental."

"I don't know," he said vaguely. "He made a few telephone calls, and here we are."

"Telephone calls?" I asked. "To whom?"

"I don't know," he said. "Does it matter?"

"Depends on who he called. You didn't hear any names?" He shook his head. "Ever hear the name 'Dupree'?"

"Just the last time you were here. Who is he?"

"I don't know. May I see Phuong?"

"Of course," he said. He rose and opened the door to the bedroom. I followed him in. Phuong was awake, her eyes bright and waiting.

"Hello, Phuong," I said. "How do you feel?"

Her lips twitched, and I smiled ruefully at her. "I know. Silly question." She nodded slightly.

"Not too long," Sergeant Jackson cautioned.

"Phuong," I said. "When I was here last, you said Muhl was looking for Molly. Why did you say that?"

She made writing motions with her fingers. I handed her my pad and pen. Laboriously, she traced the block letters: HE THINK MOLLY WORK 147 DUPREE.

"I don't understand. Do you mean he was looking for Molly at the 147 Club?"

Her eyes blinked assent.

"But you said you do not know anyone by that name."

She printed again: DUPREE KNOW. 147.

I frowned. This wasn't making sense. "What does Dupree have to do with the 147 Club?"

162

OWN.

Sergeant Jackson and I exchanged glances of disbelief.

"He owns the club? Are you sure?" She blinked "yes." "I thought that used to be the old Binh Xuyen club." She blinked again. "He bought it from them?"

Slowly, she moved her head from side to side and traced again on the pad.

SÛRETÉ.

"But . . . how . . . I . . . police?" I stammered.

She took her hand and tapped the pad significantly with her finger.

"I don't understand," I said. "How can he be *Sûreté* and not police?"

She gave me a tiny smile and handed the pad back.

"Won't you tell me, Phuong?" I asked.

She closed her eyes, and Sergeant Jackson tapped me on the arm.

"We'd better leave," he whispered. "She needs her rest."

Reluctantly, I went back into the living room. Sergeant Jackson closed the door softly behind us and leaned against the jamb.

"I don't understand," I said. "Do you? How can he be a member of the *Sûreté* and not be a policeman?"

"Different department?" he suggested.

"Maybe. But, then, how do you explain the Binh Xuyen?" I could feel the exasperation building behind my eyes.

"I don't," he said. "That's your problem. There is a connection, otherwise, she never would have suggested it. Why don't you ask him?"

"I doubt," I said drily, "if he would admit belonging to the *Sûreté*. They weren't the most popular Frenchmen in the fifties."

"Why's that?" he asked.

"They were a little careless about how they obtained

their information. In fact, I don't think there was much difference between the *Sûreté* and the *Gestapo*."

"Then why is he still in Vietnam? Isn't that a bit dangerous?"

"A bit. Do you think she's wrong?"

"Because of what happened to her?"

"Yes."

"I doubt it. She's pretty tough."

"Then we have to assume she's right, and Dupree is what she claims." I looked at my watch. It was almost five.

"I'd better go," I said. "This is not a good place to be at night."

"Yeah," he said. "The place has gone to hell since those Chinese moved in next door."

"What?"

"Just a joke. Be careful. I wouldn't put too much stock in that Lautrec's word."

He let me out and locked the door behind me. The hallway and stairwell were dark. I edged close to the wall to make my way to the street. Just before I reached the doorway, an arm snaked around my throat and bent me back. I froze in terror as the blade of a knife glinted above my eyes. Then there was a grunt, a hollow snap, and the pressure against my throat eased. The knife clattered to the floor.

I leaned weakly against the wall and turned. Ha Bo peered anxiously at me, then gave a relieved smile.

"Thank you, Ha Bo," I gasped. I looked at my assailant. At first, I thought he was lying on his face, then I realized his head had been wrenched a hundred and eighty degrees. Ha Bo flipped him over so I could see him. It was the one who had shot Tran Am.

"Lautrec's man," I said. My throat was sore and hurt when I swallowed. "He killed Tran Am. We've got to get rid of him."

Ha Bo shook his head. "Later. You go, I go. Bridge. Then," he gestured at the body.

"You'd better stay here," I said. "There may be more."

"No more. We go. Now," he insisted and took my arm. I flinched. I would have bruises there tomorrow, but at least I was alive. I wondered why Lautrec had changed his mind. Maybe it was a mistake. It had been dark in the hallway, and the dead man might have thought he had one of Phuong's guards. I would have to be more careful in the future. If I could be.

24

My neck was stiff and sore the next morning when I awoke to a pounding on the apartment door. I waited for Rachel to answer it, then remembered she had been on the night shift at MAC-V when I arrived and would not be back until later.

"Just a minute!" I yelled and swung my legs over the side of the bed. The room spun for a second, then settled, and I carefully pulled on a pair of trousers and padded barefoot to the door. I opened it and stepped hastily out of the way as Le Duc Trinh and one of his bodyguards pushed their way in. The bodyguard, that is, pushed his way in; Trinh strolled.

"Why don't you come in?" I asked sarcastically and closed the door behind them.

Trinh ignored me and gave the apartment a cursory glance before moving to the deep armchair. He pulled a handkerchief from his pocket, spread it over the cushion, and sat. He removed a gold case from an inside pocket and selected a cigarette. The bodyguard sprang to light it, then withdrew to stand silently beside the door.

"You disappoint me, Mr. Edwards," he hissed. "I thought we had an understanding."

The words were a veiled threat, but, strangely, I did not feel threatened. Disgust, yes, but the fear I had felt in his office when I went to identify Muhl's body was no longer there.

"I guess I'm just doomed to be an eternal case of

disappointment to you, Trinh," I said. "I seem to recall you using the same words to begin our last conversation. Not a very auspicious recommendation for an Oxford man."

He blinked slowly at me, a torpid lizard patiently waiting for a fly. A thin smile played around his lips.

"You seem to have undergone a metamorphosis, Mr. Edwards. Now what has caused that?"

I shrugged. "Maybe I'm just tired of being the perpetual victim, Trinh."

"Do you feel yourself to be a victim, Mr. Edwards? Is that not a vision of paranoiac self-pity?" His eyes mocked me.

"What do you want, Trinh?" I said. I crossed to the sofa and sat down. "I'm not interested in your semantic word games. Explain, then get out."

His eyes blazed briefly, then went opaque, and the smile returned to his lips.

"I'm afraid, Mr. Edwards, you have not been very discreet," he said. He pulled a slim leather notebook from a pocket and slowly flipped the pages. "Ah. Here we are. A prostitute who has disappeared since your last visit, what do you suppose has happened to her? A few drinks with a suspected *agent provocateur* at the Continental . . ."

"Dupree?" I asked in surprise. "An agent? Impossible."

"Admirable, Mr. Edwards, this art of outraged sensitivity," he murmured. "Very good. Let's see, where was I? Oh, yes. And the death of one Tran Am whose body was found floating in the river by his uncle. Incidentally," he said apologetically, "the uncle identified you as the last person to be seen with Tran Am before his unfortunate death."

He closed the notebook and carefully returned it to his pocket. He looked at me and sadly shook his head.

"I'm afraid, Mr. Edwards, that I really must insist on answers to a few questions."

"That depends upon the questions," I countered.

He nodded. "Very well. Let us begin with the prostitute."

"Which one? There are a lot of prostitutes in Saigon these days."

"Please, Mr. Edwards." He closed his eyes and gently rubbed them. "Do not make this difficult. If you recall, I warned you to stay away from the 147 Club. The one you spoke to that day. The one called 'Phuong.' "

"That is a very popular name these days," I said. "As are Suzie Wong, Helen, Betty, Mary, Ruth, Linda . . ."

"Minh," he said. "The one who is also known as Minh. The one with whom you lived for a while in 1958 when you first came to Vietnam. The one who was entertaining a colored army sergeant when you approached her. The one . . ."

"Oh, that one," I said. "Why didn't you say so in the first place? You people do your homework."

"Mr. Edwards, you are not James Bond, nor one of those famous tough American detectives. Please, let us not play roles."

"As you wish, Mr. Chan," I said. "What was the question?"

For a moment, I thought he was going to order his bodyguard on me. The skin over his forehead and cheekbones tightened until I thought his skull was going to burst through. With an effort, he forced himself into control and gave a short, hollow laugh.

"Very good, Mr. Edwards. Very good."

"One tries," I said modestly. His lips tightened fractionally. "Sorry. You were saying?"

"We would like to visit with this prostitute friend of yours. Unfortunately, she has disappeared. I do not suppose you would have any idea where we might find her?"

168

I shook my head. "Sorry. I'm afraid I can't help you. In fact, if you do find her, I wish you'd let me know. She was going to try and find someone for me, but I haven't spoken with her since that night." It wasn't exactly a lie, to speak with someone implies a two-way conversation. Over the years I have often found that the best way to avoid giving answers you do not wish to give is to stay as close to the truth as possible. Somehow, that gives the timbre of your voice a hint of honesty.

"You're quite sure?" he asked.

I nodded.

"Who was the individual she was trying to contact?"

I could see nothing wrong in giving his name. Besides, something told me Trinh already knew and was using the question to see if I was playing games with him.

"Lautrec," I said.

"Why did you wish to speak to him?"

"I still do," I said, sidestepping the small snare. "I believe he was one of the last to see Muhl alive."

"How do you know that?"

"I don't. That's why I wish to speak with him."

"I see." He pursed his lips and gently tapped them with manicured fingertips while he considered me.

"Anything else?" I asked politely.

"Yes," he said. "The matter of Mr. Dupree."

"Sorry. I thought he was a broker. I believe he owns a warehouse on the Quay Lemoine."

"What has he spoken about when you were together?"

"I don't remember," I said. "Just idle conversation about the war and politics and books. You know, the type of converstaion normal over a friendly drink together. Are you sure of your information about him? Sometimes, during questioning, certain people will say what they think you want to hear. Surely you have encountered that before?"

I was heartened at the indecision that flitted over his face. If I didn't miss my guess, the information he had on

169

Dupree had been wrung out of someone in the interrogation cells, and Trinh was too intelligent to place total reliance on anything learned under those circumstances.

"Perhaps our informant erred," he said.

"Maybe you should ask him again," I ventured. "He could have mistaken the name."

"Unfortunately, he has died. A heart attack, I believe."

"That's too bad," I said. "It must be the tension of the time."

"Yes," he said. "An unfortunate accident. Much like the one that claimed your friend Tran Am, I should think. I believe you were the last to see him alive?"

"I don't know," I said. "We parted company in Dakow." Again, not the whole truth, but enough of it to lend credibility to my words.

"What were you doing in Dakow?"

"Looking for Phuong. But that is an impossible place to find anyone."

"Yes," he agreed. "They are most uncooperative there."

The door opened, and Rachel, her arms full of shopping bags, stepped into the room. She stopped and looked from the bodyguard to Trinh to me. A loaf of French bread poked from the top of one bag. She blinked, hesitated, then moved forward, and gave me a perfunctory kiss on the cheek.

"I'm sorry, darling," she said brightly. "I didn't know you were busy." She crossed to the table and placed the bags upon it.

"This is Mr. Trinh," I said formally. "Mr. Trinh, Rachel Holmes."

"How do you do?" she said and extended her hand. He rose and politely touched her hand with his fingertips.

"My pleasure, Miss Holmes," he replied.

"Is Con doing a story on you, Mr. Trinh?" she asked and returned to sit on the arm of the sofa beside me.

"I do not believe so," he replied. "At least, I hope not."

"I never thought of that," I said. "You know, Mr. Trinh, you might just make a good story. Mr. Trinh's a policeman," I said, turning to Rachel, "a very good policeman."

"I have had a small degree of success," Trinh said. "But," he added pointedly, "there are other stories I am sure your readers would prefer. Please excuse me. I must be going."

"I'm sorry I couldn't be of more help to you, Mr. Trinh," I said and climbed to my feet. I followed him to the door.

"There will be another time," he said. "After all, is not the third time the charmed time? There is a lot of truth in the old clichés. Goodbye, Miss Holmes. Perhaps we'll meet again when I have more time."

"Perhaps, Mr. Trinh," she said brightly. "I'll look forward to it."

He nodded and left. The bodyguard followed and carefully closed the door behind him. I drew a deep breath and let it out slowly.

"I don't think," Rachel said slowly, "that I would care to meet him again."

"You wouldn't," I said. I yawned and winced at the twinge of pain. She looked at me closely.

"What happened to you?"

"An accident," I said and told her about Ha Bo saving my life. "Apparently," I concluded, "Lautrec has decided I'm expendable after all."

"Why do you suppose he did that?" she said. "Did you find out anything?" She crossed to the table, picking up the bags and carrying them to the tiny kitchenette where she began to unpack.

"No, not much," I said. I went to the bathroom and began to work up a lather in my shaving cup. "That's why Trinh was here."

171

"Are you sure?" she called.

"What do you mean?" I began to spread the lather on my face.

"Something made Lautrec change his mind. Something you did before you went back to Dakow."

"Maybe he was simply trying to find Phuong," I said. "Maybe it was a case of mistaken identity. It was dark in the hallway."

She came to the bathroom and leaned against the door, watching me as I began to draw the razor through the lather.

"You don't really believe that," she said.

"No," I said.

"What else did you do?"

"I checked one of Muhl's last assignments," I said. "One I had given him after he suppressed that story of mine on Major Powell. The consolidation of the PX warehouses."

"Why that one?"

I finished shaving and bent to rinse the excess soap from my face. "It was the nearest assignment that no other news service bothered with."

"What did you find out?"

"The move was a good one efficiency-wise, but as news value it's as mundane now as it was then."

"Then where did you go?"

"I met Dupree at the Continental for a drink, then went to Dakow. You know the rest."

I splashed cologne on my cheeks and moved past her to the wardrobe. I slipped out of my trousers and pulled a fresh pair of twills and a bush shirt from the wardrobe and began to dress.

"You're sure that's all?" she asked. She crossed to the liquor cabinet and poured a small Scotch.

I shrugged. "Nothing else. Except Molly."

"Who's she?"

"I don't know. Do you?"

172

"She might be a nurse," she said thoughtfully. "I can check. Do you think she's involved in this somehow?"

"Probably. But, for the life of me, I can't see how. Unless she's running drugs. No one has heard of her. Muhl was looking for her. At least," I added, "that was what Phuong discovered. Maybe she was just someone Muhl was seeing."

"No," she said thoughtfully. "Muhl wasn't seeing her."

"How do you know that?" I asked suspiciously.

"Because he would know where to find her if he was," she said calmly. "Are you sure you can't give me any more to go on?"

"Positive," I said. I sat on the edge of the bed to pull on my socks.

"Then it has to be either Dupree or the warehouse," she said decidedly.

"How do you figure?" I couldn't find a shoe and bent to look under the bed.

"You said so the other night after Lautrec killed Tran Am. Remember? Your friends weren't safe, but you were, as long as you didn't get too close? Or words to that effect."

I rose from the floor and sat slowly upon the bed and stared at her thoughtfully.

"Apparently, you got too close," she finished. "The only question is: which one is it? The warehouse or Dupree?"

"Or both?" I said slowly. "What if they're connected somehow? The warehouse to Dupree and Dupree to Lautrec?"

Something began to stir in my mind like morning fog over the Rung Sat swamps, but I couldn't focus upon it. The connecting premise was missing from the syllogism. I had everything except the link. What did all three have in common?

"I don't think so," Rachel said. "Dupree and Lautrec

173

are both French, but there the similarity ends. What could they possibly have in common other than that?"

"What did you say?" the fog began to swirl faster.

"I said 'Dupree and Lautrec are both French . . .' "

"And where was Bay Vien given refuge?" I interjected.

A small smile tugged at the corners of her mouth.

"France," she said and raised her glass in mock salute.

25

As I sat on the Continental terrace and watched Dupree weave his way through the noon throng towards me, I told myself it was not a classic syllogism worthy of Aristotle, but rather a syllogism born from *hysterico passio*, an instinct founded on the barest of evidence. Still, it was the only link visible, even though it might be strictly coincidental.

With a jolt, I remembered a few months previous when Muhl and I had sat at this same table and vehemently argued the value of coincidence.

"There are times, Con, when you have to work purely on speculation," he said.

"Work, yes," I answered. "But do not expect to print speculations. You have no proof that Phan Xuan An is working for the Vietcong."

His lips tightened, and he threw himself back in his chair in exasperation and glared at me. He had just come from the office, where he discovered I had killed his story claiming Reuters correspondent Phan Xuan An was an undercover agent for the enemy forces. He had assembled a libelous exposé indicting the reporter. Muhl based his suppositions on a series of coincidences in which An, a frequent dinner guest at the Presidential Palace, had reportedly been seen in the company of Colonel Bei Tin, a notorious former leader of the Viet-minh faction and currently suspected of running a cell of spies. Muhl had no quotes on the record from reputable sources, no photographs, and no evidence on anything of a military or political nature having been passed between them, even if the rumor of their meeting was true.

"That is what is being said on the streets," he insisted stubbornly. "And he is under investigation."

"According to a file clerk at USIS," I said drily. "These are the same people who are claiming we'll be home for Christmas. What's the matter with you? Can't you see the danger of what you wrote? Where is your evidence? Reuters would sue our asses off without evidence and rightly so. We'd be lucky to find work as bellhops at Raffles in Singapore. Personally, I'm too old to be in the job market."

"That's why I was sent to be your legs," he said. "You're getting old. Maybe your judgement is also getting old. Did you think of that?"

"Maybe. But I doubt it." I could feel the anger building in me and fought to keep it under control. "And that's immaterial. I killed the story and thoroughly intend to let it stay dead. That, despite my age, is still my option, my right, as bureau chief."

"Good afternoon. Or should I say 'good evening.' " Dupree halted in front of my table and consulted the thin Patek watch on his wrist. "How were the briefings?"

"The usual song and dance. Troop increases up forty-seven percent. More fodder. Please join me. I'd like to talk with you about an idea," I said. I could feel Muhl's spectre grinning over my shoulder.

"My pleasure. Are you buying?" He sat and signaled a waiter to bring him a cassis and water.

"Yes. The last of the big-time spenders," I said. "Are you sure you won't have something more substantial?"

"Thank you, no," he said. "I have some business to contend with later and must keep a straight head."

"With Lautrec?" I suggested gently.

"I beg your pardon?" His face was smooth and bland,

176

but I felt the sudden tension emanating from his body, similar to the tension a forest animal emits when it feels threatened.

"Your business this evening, would it by any chance be with Lautrec?"

"What are you suggesting, my friend?" The slight emphasis on 'friend' and his hands moving restlessly upon the table belied his outwardly calm composure.

"Suggesting? Nothing. Why do you avoid the question?"

"Why do you ask it?"

I shrugged and reached for my drink. I sipped slowly and waited on him. His eyes shifted from me to the square to the bartender and waiter and back again to me.

"Lautrec is an animal. Really, Con, this is most unfair of you. Suppose someone overheard you?"

"He's French," I said. "Partly, at any rate. Perhaps a little *bon homme?*"

"Please," he began.

"Why don't we stop this verbal fencing, Dupree? Lautrec seems to always be in the right place at the right time. Why? And how? Most important, how did he know I saw Phuong?"

"This is a city of intrigue. You must expect to be followed when you begin looking for certain answers," he said. He lifted his glass from its saucer, sipped, and replaced it. "And everyone knows that Le Duc Trinh has taken a special interest in you."

"True," I admitted. "But how would he know what I asked Phuong at the 147 Club?"

"Perhaps you were overheard."

"I'm sure of it," I said. "But whoever overheard me was on your payroll. You own the 147 Club."

"Ah. I see. Guilty by association. Con, this is beneath you. First, you suggest I'm a policeman, now I'm an associate of Lautrec. Which is it?"

"Perhaps both," I said slowly.

He gave me a contemptuous look and pushed himself away from the table.

"I think you better give up this crusade," he said. "You are becoming paranoid. Simply because I own the 147 Club does not mean that I have total control over my employees. You received information from Phuong. Why could not someone else likewise get information?"

"Highly possible," I said. "But how would Muhl have known who to contact for information? He had not been around long enough to know who to approach in such matters. Except you, Dupree. What did you tell him? Why did you tell him? What was he working on?"

He rose from the table and looked down at me. His eyes were flat and accusing like the eyes of gray old men whose advice goes unheeded.

"You are making a big mistake," he said softly. "I hope it will not be a tragic one."

He threw a few bills on the table.

"I do not want you to pay for my drinks," he said and left.

I watched him cross Lam Lon Square and disappear down Tu Do Street. I had no more pieces to the puzzle, but inductively I could make a few guesses. But the coldness in my stomach made me wonder if I had not erred in making him angry. I did not like his gesture at the end: it was too final.

26

"YOU'VE GOT NOTHING," Sergeant Jackson said bluntly. We were sitting across from each other at the table in the sitting room in Cholon. Phuong was asleep in the other room when I arrived. I took the opportunity to tell him about my meeting with Dupree.

"In fact," he continued, "that was very stupid. If he is involved in this, then you've just put him on his guard. Why did you do it?"

"What else could I have done? Either nobody knows what Muhl was working on (and I can't believe that because somebody went to a hell of a lot of trouble to shut him up), or else everybody knows except me. Everywhere I turn I run into stone walls."

"Maybe you should just drop it."

"I can't." I looked involuntarily at the door to the room where Phuong lay. "I've gone too far now."

"True," he said. "Maybe we should just find this Lautrec and settle it."

"Exterminate with extreme prejudice?" I said sourly and shook my head. "We'd still not know anything."

"The truth is that important?"

"What else is there?" I said and wearily rose to my feet and left.

"Let's go over it again," Rachel said.

Moths butted against the lone lamp on my desk. I could barely see her in the shadows just outside the lamp's glow.

"There's nothing to go over," I said. "Dupree said nothing and admitted nothing."

"But by doing so, he intimated his involvement."

"Which leaves us nowhere. Even if he is involved with Lautrec we don't know in what or why. And we still don't have the link between them and Muhl."

"It has to be something with the warehouse story he covered," she said. "What did you do with those charts Captain what's-his-name gave you?"

"They're on the desk," I said.

She rose, crossed to the desk, and shuffled books and papers around until she found them. She returned to her chair and began to go over them.

"You won't find anything," I said. "Those reports are models of efficiency."

"Ummm. Maybe. But then again, maybe they are too efficient."

"Oh? You have found something? Things are not the way they seem?"

"Look," she said and brought the papers to me. She knelt beside the arm of my chair.

"Here are the figures from PX sales from the four warehouses before the consolidation and after the consolidation. Note there is roughly a thirty-percent increase."

"Twenty-nine point five, to be precise," I said.

"Shut up. Orders have also increased thirty-five percent."

"Most efficient. Like I said."

"*But,*" she said, "troop increases in the country are up over forty-seven percent according to your briefing this afternoon. Why aren't the PX figures coordinately higher?"

"Maybe some don't use the PX."

She gave me a withering look and said, "How many soldiers don't use the only store open to them in their

180

areas? And look at this." She reshuffled the papers and placed another chart in my lap. "PX orders are forty percent larger. That is, the dock orders, the bills of lading for the central warehouse, are up forty percent. That leaves ten point five percent unaccounted for, while gross receipts have climbed thirty-three percent. Con, none of the figures correspond. With a forty-seven percent troop increase, the gross receipts for PX sales should have been much higher. At least ten percent more, and that's a bottom-line figure. It could even be seventeen percent or the difference between PX orders plus troop increase and sales increase. What does that suggest?"

"The black market? But there are many possible reasons for the discrepancy in the figures. KIAs, MIAs, fluctuating costs in wholesale and shipping increases, just to name a few. What else do we have?"

"What else could Muhl have been working on?" she countered.

Our eyes met, and we both knew that although it wasn't the answer, at least we had the key piece in the puzzle. We still didn't know what Muhl was doing at the plantation when he was killed, or how Dupree and Lautrec fitted into the scheme, but at least we had direction. Maybe we could even find the elusive Molly.

The shadows in the room suddenly seemed ominous, the air heavy and thick. I reached behind me to click on the floor lamp and rose to start the ceiling fan. I felt a strange exhilaration and told myself I should talk with Colonel Black again, but I knew it was too late for that.

27

THERE WERE NO stars and no moon and the wind across the Quay Lemoine had a damp chill to it that suggested monsoon rains not far behind. I huddled closer to the stone of the entryway to the Lotus Bar across the street from Dupree's warehouse. I wished I had worn something heavier than the bush jacket I had on and tried again to read my watch, but it was too dark. I guessed I had been in the doorway two hours, which would make it almost one a.m., well past curfew. I sighed and jumped as Sergeant Jackson spoke from the darkness behind me.

"Will you for Christ's sake be still?" he whispered. "You want them to hear you?"

"I'm cold," I whispered back.

"Jesus Christ."

"Make much noise. No should," Ha Bo said accusingly. "Bad mans here."

"He's right," Jackson said.

"Oh, shut up," I growled and turned my attention back to the warehouse. I was miserable, but took comfort from their presence and silently blessed Rachel, who had insisted I take them with me while she stayed with Phuong. I thought we would have trouble getting them to leave Phuong, but days of staying cooped up in the small room had worn on Jackson's nerves, and trying to keep Ha Bo from the "bad mans" was next to impossible. That, however, also worried me, for if we discovered what I hoped to discover, I wasn't sure I'd be able to control him. We had only Jackson's .45 for armament.

I felt again for my camera and wondered if the single

bulb over the warehouse door was providing enough light for the star-scope lens. I also wondered if I wasn't jumping to conclusions. Maybe Dupree had meant legitimate business. Maybe he and the others had already been and gone. Maybe he was home fast asleep in his comfortable bed while we stood in this cold doorway in the harsh wind and caught pneumonia.

I jerked my thoughts away from self-pity as Jackson's hand squeezed my bicep, then pointed down the street.

At first, I saw nothing, then two slits of light. Jackson's breath was warm on the back of my neck as he leaned close and whispered.

"Blackout lights. Army truck."

I nodded that I understood and kept my eyes on the slits of light. My stomach began to roll, and I fought back the nausea that threatened to make me vomit. Slowly, I brought the camera to my eye and looked through the lens. I needn't have worried: the light from the lone bulb was enough for the star-scope. I could see the truck and the markings that identified it as U.S. Army, but I could only see the outline of the driver and passenger. I lowered the camera and moved to the rear of the entryway with Jackson and Ha Bo.

"It's one of ours," I whispered. "But I can't tell who's driving or riding shotgun."

"Is bad mans?" Ha Bo asked.

"Yes," I said, "but . . . wait!"

I was too late. A terrible sigh that made the back of my neck cold slipped from his lips, and he was gone. I blinked. I had heard nothing, seen nothing, only sensed a large shadow moving against my night vision.

"Where'd he go?" I whispered to Jackson.

"I don't know, but I'm glad he's on our side. What now?"

"Wait until the truck gets to the door. Maybe there'll be enough light there."

I moved back to the front of the entryway and again

raised the camera. I thought of Loan executing the suspected Vietcong terrorist and how I had missed the picture. This time, I would be prepared. And I was. Everything would have been perfect except I hadn't counted on the warehouse door swinging open from the inside, and the truck rolling through without stopping. Instantly, the doors closed behind it, and I was left without a photo.

28

"Damn," I said softly and lowered the camera. Any fear still lurking within my soul dissipated with the rush of anger and frustration at missing the picture. I slammed my palm against the concrete entryway.

"Hey," whispered Jackson urgently. "Keep the noise down."

"It doesn't matter," I said crossly. "I missed them."

"What?"

"I didn't get the picture."

"Why the hell not?"

"Someone was waiting for them. The truck didn't stop."

He swore softly, long, and fluently.

"I know," I answered. "But I thought they would have to stop to open the damn door."

"Maybe there's a window. In the back," he muttered doubtfully.

"Oh, yes," I said sarcastically. "And maybe a patio with French doors and a major-domo to bring us a pink gin while we set up lights for a decent portrait."

"Never know until we look."

"Across that?" I gestured at the vacant space in front of us.

"If you truly want this."

"You know, I've been meaning to tell you that at times, you sound like Hemingway."

"Faulkner," he said. "The first black Faulkner. Let's go."

"I think Baldwin's already beaten you to that title," I muttered.

I crouched as low as I could and scuttled across the dark street after him. I flattened myself against the warehouse, my heart fluttering like a bird with a broken wing, waiting for discovery and the shot. Time seemed to become unhinged, and suddenly I found myself back at Hue, standing in one of the darkened windows across the street watching the counterattack upon the Citadel. For all my flippancy, I was more frightened than I had been in the initial confrontation with Lautrec when Tran Am was killed. At least then, I had seen the danger, known direction, and was located in the time-space continuum. But here, I was adrift in a murky sea, blinded to all around me.

Perhaps Muhl was right: maybe I had been too distant from the war, too distant from the second horseman, a watcher from the shadows who countered his lack of involvement with protective shields of colorful prose.

"There is no substitute for the real thing," Muhl said. "How can you write about the stench of death, the fear of the unexpected, if you never stood in a jungle clearing with hot urine running down your leg?"

"The same way I can look at a fine painting by Goya, or Degas, or Wyeth and write about the passion within my heart."

We were sitting in my apartment and drinking beaded glasses of gin and tonic against the heat. The fans turned sluggishly overhead, and the cries of the vendors on the street below were muted and dispirited.

Four weeks had passed since his affair with Rachel, during which time we had not spoken except during chance encounters in the office. I had just arrived at the apartment and was in the process of mixing a drink when he knocked at the door.

"What do you want?" I said rudely.

"To talk," he answered and spread his fingers, palms toward me, disarmingly. "Just talk. Nothing more."

"I'm not sure we have anything to talk about," I said. "Besides, I haven't much time. We're going out to eat at the Mekong."

"One drink," he said. "Then I'll go."

"Come in," I said grudgingly. "One drink, then out."

"Thank you," he said. He entered and shut the door behind him. He walked to the center of the room and looked around him.

"I never could understand why you insist upon living here."

"Don't start that," I said. "I'm comfortable here. The ambiance suits me."

"True," he answered and took the drink I proferred from my outstretched hand. He moved to the easy chair by the floor lamp and sat. "It's romantic."

"Look, I know you can't help being insulting, you probably don't even know you are, but do try to be civilized. What did you want to talk about?"

I crossed to the balcony and looked down into the street. It was so hot that practically no one moved on the street. Even the leaves of the trees drooped hot and dusty from the branches. A movement caught my eye: a man standing in the doorway of the bookseller across the street, his white suit dappled with shadows from the leaves on the trees.

"You know, that night when she came to me, I knew she didn't come because she loved me. She came for you. I only wish someone loved me as much."

"I don't want to hear your history, Muhl," I said absently, keeping my attention on the doorway.

"You know, you've never called me by my first name. Why don't you?"

"I'll stick with Muhl. First names are for intimates. I don't want to be friends with you."

He lifted the glass from the table, sipped from it, and replaced it on the table. I looked back at the white-suited figure across the street. I could feel his eyes watching me.

"I'm sorry," he said behind me. "I wish we could start over. I wish we could be friends."

"Friends?" I turned to him. His face was shiny with perspiration, and his open-necked shirt patchy with wetness. His stateside haircut had disappeared, and his hair now touched the tops of his ears. A certain weariness showed in his face, the pouches under his eyes, the deep lines at the corners of his mouth. The brash young man who had approached me at the Continental months ago and announced he was to be "my legs" had disappeared.

"How can we be friends?"

"I don't know," he said. He gestured miserably, then grabbed his drink, and drained it. He rattled the ice in the glass and stared at it for a minute. I waited. It was his visit. "May I have another?"

"Help yourself," I said absently. He rose and crossed to the liquor table. I heard the bottle of Gordon's gurgle, then the snap of the ice as the gin washed over it. Why, I wondered, was he standing down there? What was he waiting for?

"What do you want?" I said aloud. Muhl thought I was speaking to him and answered.

"Let me have a chance. That's all. Let me have a chance and . . . ," he hesitated. I faced him again.

"And . . . ," I prompted.

"Let me work on other things. I don't care what." He hurried to stave off my retort. "Anything. At least, let me look. Human-interest features, let me take a few

188

patrols, anything. I'm a writer, damn it, not a two-bit hack tied to obits."

I sighed. "It still comes back to your career, doesn't it?"

"No. Yes. It's part of it. I need to be something more than I am. Like . . . ," he fumbled for words.

"Salt and pepper?" I suggested.

He gave me a wry grin and said, "Same old Con. Pedantic as hell."

"Maybe," I said and swirled my drink in its glass. "But it buys the groceries."

"It's not the truth."

"Truth is a vagrant," I said. "That's something else you have to learn."

"Or you unlearn. There is no substitute for the real thing. How can you write about the stench of death, the fear of the unexpected, if you've never stood in a jungle clearing with hot urine running down your leg?"

"The same way I can look at a fine painting by Goya, or Degas, or Wyeth and write about the passion within my heart."

He grinned sheepishly. "Purple prose is catching, isn't it?"

"You're learning," I replied. "You might have a chance yet."

"If you give it to me," he countered swiftly.

I looked down at the tiny bits of ice in my drink. He was right, more right then he knew. It wouldn't be long until the *Times* began to wonder why their fair-headed boy wasn't producing and begin to query.

"There's nothing at the moment except a press junket to Nha Trang," I said. "Do you want that?"

"It would be a change," he said.

"Okay. You can have it."

"And how about features?"

"Any ideas?"

"I have an idea about something. It might be nothing, but I'd like to check it out."

"What is it?"

"I'd rather not say until I have more information. It's a long shot."

"Go ahead. But be careful. Remember: there's damn few rules here."

"I'll remember. Thanks." He hastened from the room before I could change my mind. I listened to his footsteps on the stairs as I crossed to the balcony. The man was still there. I saluted him with my glass as Muhl stepped into the street. The man moved from the doorway and looked up at me. Even from that distance I could see his eyes, the sharpness of his features. He gave me a tiny smile, nodded, then walked rapidly away towards Lam Lon Square about thirty paces behind Muhl. I raised my glass to my lips, but it was empty, and I turned back to the liquor table.

"Come on," Jackson whispered urgently. "We can't stand here all night."

"Right behind you," I mumbled and followed him as he darted around the corner of the warehouse and ducked down an alley. I moved carefully, grateful for the darkness that kept me from seeing the filth that oozed beneath my shoes. I gagged as the smell rose from the bed of the alley and hung in putrescent clouds in the narrow space safe from dissipating winds. I barked my shin against a wooden crate and halted, fearful of the sudden movement and squeals from within the crate. I could no longer see Jackson, and for one insane moment the tasteless Rastus jokes flashed through my mind. Then I sensed him beside me and felt his hand upon my arm and dutifully moved in the direction of his insistent tug. Cautiously, we crabbed our way down the alley. We stopped below a dim rectangle three feet over our heads.

"Kneel," Jackson commanded in a soft whisper.

"Like hell," I shot back. "You kneel."

"I've got the pistol," he said patiently.

I knelt, my stomach heaving, as my hands slid into slick, rotting garbage. Tiny insects began to bite my hands, and a small furry creature tried to mount my wrist. I almost went face first into the mess as Jackson's weight flew from the small of my back. I rose and placed my shoulder beneath his feet. I heard a small creak as he eased the window open, then he pulled himself up and into the warehouse.

"Give me your hand."

I raised my arms and moved them back and forth. His hands closed tightly on my wrists, and I was unceremoniously hauled up and through the window like a sack of flour. My chest scraped painfully across the sill, and then I was inside, standing next to Jackson.

Light shone through a crack at the bottom of a door, and I could see we were in some kind of storeroom filled with large crates. Cautiously, we tiptoed across the floor, testing the planks carefully before placing our weight upon them. Jackson placed his ear against the door, then gently eased it open a crack, and peered through.

"Can't see anything except crates," he said. He tugged the door wider and slipped inside. I followed and found myself in a narrow aisle between walls of crates that stretched to an unseen ceiling. The writing on one of the crates read NIKON, another REVLON, and still a third WALKER & SONS, LTD./ SCOTCH WHISKY.

We crept down the aisle and peered around the corner of a crate and found the truck, Sergeant Bowman, Lautrec, and Dupree. Shadowy silent figures were quickly unloading boxes of shaving cream, cases of beer, cigarettes, nylons, radios, and God help me, Spam from the truck.

Lautrec silently handed Bowman an envelope while

Dupree stood off to the side and noted the contents with a gold pen on a small pad as they were off-loaded. Bowman thumbed through the contents, then shook his head, and stuffed the envelope in his back pocket.

"The boss says that's not enough," he drawled. The Tennessee accent sounded strange and false in the near silence. "He says another thousand."

Lautrec shook his head. "That is most unfortunate. Perhaps with penicillin, but not for this." He gestured contemptuously at the freight.

"We ain't a fucking hospital," Bowman said. "That's all you get."

"And that, my friend, is all you get. The market is not as demanding as it was once. Too many of your countrymen are trading."

"Nickels and dimes," Bowman scoffed. "We bring you bulk. Another thousand."

Lautrec shrugged and shook his head and placed his hands in the pockets of his jacket. The right pocket bulged ominously; the movement was not lost upon Bowman. He shifted a wad from his right to left cheek and contemptuously spat a brown stream onto the concrete floor.

"Don't threaten me, you little shit," he said. "Another thousand or that's the last load. Take it or leave it."

Dupree moved to Lautrec's side and whispered in his ear. They withdrew a little distance from Bowman and began to talk earnestly.

Jackson nudged me, and I carefully turned my head to look at him. His face gleamed with perspiration. He looked at the camera around my neck, then flicked his eyes at the people in front of us. His meaning was clear: take the damn picture, and let's get out of here!

Lautrec left Dupree and returned to Bowman. He eyed him for a moment. I had to admire Bowman's calm. I had looked into those eyes myself when they weren't all that angry.

192

"There is no more money," he said softly. Bowman made an uncomplimentary remark and started to turn away.

"But maybe we could make a trade?"

Bowman turned back to him. I could see the interest, cold and calculating, in his eyes.

"What kind of trade?" he asked suspiciously.

"Heroin," Lautrec said. He kept his eyes on Bowman's face, his hands in his pocket.

"Horse?" Bowman eased the cud from his cheek and dropped it onto the floor.

"You could make much more from the heroin than the thousand you ask for." It was the first time Dupree had spoken. There was no bantering edge to his voice like he used at the Continental, no suavity, no cultured resonance. It was harsh and commanding, filled with the arrogance of one in control.

"Yeah. I could," Bowman said. "I could also waste my life instead of five years if I'm caught."

"Then do not get caught," Dupree said. "Is not reward comparable to risk?"

Bowman scratched his head and looked thoughtful. Slowly, he nodded.

"All right with me," he said. "But I have to talk to the boss."

"By all means," Dupree said. "We will give you one kilo a load, uncut. That should be a fair trade."

"I dunno," Bowman said. He pulled a plug of tobacco from his pocket and bit off a chunk. He chewed thoughtfully for a minute, then shook his head.

"You're outta my league," he confessed. "That'll be up to the boss."

"Very well," Dupree said. "Let us know."

"Wait," Bowman said, as Dupree began to move away from him. "I gotta know where the exchange will take place."

Lautrec moved suddenly to Bowman's right, placing

the American between himself and Dupree. Dupree looked steadily at him for a long moment before speaking.

"Why?"

"I want everything laid out before I report. Simple promises ain't enough. How do I know you can deliver?"

"You have my word."

"Ahuh." Bowman unleashed another stream of brown juice that narrowly missed Lautrec's white shoes. "Have a hard time sticking that under the mattress, won't I?"

Tiny muscles moved in Dupree's jaw. He looked at Lautrec. He nodded, and Dupree gave Bowman a chilly smile. He reached into his pocket, removed a small vial, and tossed it to Bowman.

"A small down payment," he said. "The rest on delivery."

Bowman removed the rubber stopper from the vial, moistened the tip of a finger, touched it to the white powder in the vial, and tasted it. He nodded, replaced the stopper, and dropped it into his pocket.

"Okay," he said quietly. "And, if the boss says so, where'll I deliver? Here?"

"No," Dupree answered. "This has been used too often for business of this nature. We will take delivery on the sixteenth at the Michelin Plantation."

I gave a start, and Jackson's fingers dug into my shoulder. I shrugged them off and raised the camera and pressed the shutter as Bowman stepped forward, hand outstretched, to seal the bargain.

It was the wrong time to take a picture. I had not noticed the men had finished unloading the truck, and the shutter snapped loudly in the silence. The men froze, then Lautrec whirled to face our direction. His hands slipped from his pockets, the right clutching a small automatic.

194

"Jesus Christ," Jackson said and pulled me out of the way. I heard a click as he thumbed the safety off the .45.

"Get the hell out of here. Quick!" he said and fired at a shadowy figure on his left. The shot was thunderous in the closed space, but I heard a cry, as his bullet found its mark, then the clatter of a rifle falling to the floor.

"Move!" he screamed and gave me another shove as a fusillade of bullets struck the crate behind which we hid. The figures began to move towards us, then a dark cloud dropped down upon them. It was Ha Bo. I heard a scream, then one of the figures flew through the air and crashed unmoving to the floor in front of Lautrec. Then another screeched in fear, a terrible animal sound, and they began to mill in confusion, firing at shadows, as Ha Bo disappeared between a pile of crates. The engine of the truck roared, and I caught a brief glimpse of Bowman's tight face behind the wheel as the truck crashed through the doors and roared away. I looked for Lautrec and Dupree, but they had disappeared. Then Jackson was pulling me down the aisle, back the way we came.

"Ha Bo," I protested as he threw me towards the window and turned to fire two shots through the doorway.

"Gone!" he yelled, and I flew through the window and landed on all fours in the garbage-covered alley. He dropped lightly beside me and pulled me up, and we raced down the alley to the back of the warehouse and out onto the pier of the Quay Lemoine. I could see the water rippling in front of us and hear it lapping against the pier. I thought for a moment that we were going to jump, but Jackson turned and we ran down the street paralleling the river, our shoes slapping frantically on the pavement. My lungs began to burn with the effort of trying to keep up, while perspiration rolled off my forehead and stung my eyes. My legs began to wobble, then he dodged down a side street, made another turn, and I saw the park looming before us. We ran into the park, dodged between the trees, then slipped behind a privet hedge, and dropped to the cool grass. I rolled to my back and stared at the sky and wished I could hear something besides the thumping in my temples and my lungs gasping for air.

"I think we've lost them," Jackson said shortly. He sat up and faced me.

"Did you get what you wanted?"

"Yeah," I managed and sat up. I swallowed heavily. My mouth tasted of brass.

"The only trouble is, what do I do with it?"

29

THE GENTLE RAIN that marked the beginning of the monsoon season had begun to fall, giving blessed relief from the stifling heat that had marked the past few days. The apartment was cool, and Jackson sat like an ebony Buddha in the far corner and watched the battle raging between Rachel and me in the middle of the room.

Two days had passed since our visit to the warehouse on the Quay Lemoine, two days in which the city had grown silent to all my efforts at finding either Dupree or Lautrec. No one seemed to know where they had gone, but I could tell by the wavering eyes and hesitant answers to my questions that our involvement in the affair was common knowledge. Saigon was that way, though; there were no secrets, and when I walked the streets I could feel dark eyes on my back like rifle sights on a bull's-eye.

"You have the picture," Rachel said again. "What more do you need? Turn it over to the authorities."

I sighed and tried again to explain. Pictures could be altered, but even if the picture was believed, what did it show that was condemning? Dupree shaking hands with Sergeant Bowman and the back of a white-suited figure in the foreground. By any stretch of the imagination it could be nothing more than innocuous. Dupree was not wanted by the police, indeed quite the opposite: his wit and repartee were in constant demand at Presidental Palace soirees, for he avoided politics at all costs. In the political wars that raged constantly in Saigon government circles, this made him a "safe" guest at whom no faction could point an accusing finger.

"Then give the picture to Colonel Black. Let the Americans do something about it."

Again, what could they do? Sergeant Bowman's presence could easily be explained as public relations, since the U.S. had been trying for years to instill the precepts of town-hall democracy into an agrarian culture thousands of years old. Since Dupree was a broker, it would be only natural to assume he was involved in the rural pacification program in which the military helped to build schools and public facilities in an attempt to present alternate democratic solutions to communist problems. But the peasants didn't want books and buildings, their wants were simpler: more food. Rice. It is hard for a man to be philosophically idealistic on an empty stomach. Still, the U.S. tried, and by day the schools went up and by night came down and directives had gone out to all military personnel to smile, smile, smile, and walk softly around the Vietnamese. We were, after all, guests in their country, and all needed to spread the good word as democratic evangelists. And that was precisely what Bowman appeared to be doing shaking Dupree's hand in the picture.

"But the stolen PX supplies . . ."

". . . will have been moved by now."

"And the heroin?"

"What heroin? Another invention by a correspondent looking for an exposé. No," I said, "we know, but that's not enough. What with this new pacification program, the last thing the military and government want is a scandal. Remember my story on Major Powell?"

"That's only part of it, though, isn't it?"

I did not say anything.

"You still don't know who killed Muhl."

She was right: Muhl's ghost was still with me. I could

still see him lying on the metal tray in the refrigerated room at the police station. It was a mean way for anyone to die, and I couldn't forget that or forgive whoever had done that to him.

"You know what you are?" she said to my silence. "You are a twentieth-century Don Quixote."

"But think of the honor," I tried to joke. She shook her head tiredly and turned away.

"Oh, go ahead. Just don't expect me here when you get back."

"I'm sorry," I said and tried to put my hands on her shoulders, but she angrily shook them off and left the room without speaking.

I stood in the middle of the awkward silence for a minute to see if she would relent and return. She didn't, and finally I looked at Jackson still sitting quietly in the corner of the room.

"What do you think?"

He shrugged, rose, and stretched, then ambled to the liquor cabinet. He reached for the bottle of Scotch and poured a heavy drink. He ignored the soda siphon.

"Best leave now. I don't want to be on the roads at night."

"Do you think they'll be waiting for us?"

"Wouldn't you?" He tossed the drink down and set the glass firmly upside down on the table. "That much and no more. Until we return."

"If we return," I amended quietly.

"That, too," he said.

30

THE RAINS HAD begun in earnest by the time we reached the outskirts of the Michelin Plantation, but Jackson viewed that development as a good sign as he drove the stolen jeep off the road and into the first grove of rubber trees. The Michelin Plantation was actually like a province unto itself. Several small villages, actually palm-thatched barrack huts built to house the thousands of workers, spread out like the spokes of a wheel from the central mansion built during the French occupation. Each grove had its own overseer and workers who were by now back in their huts out of the blinding rain. In the old days, this would not have been true, for the peasants would have been forced to work on through the storm. But since the end of the French rule, working conditions had changed drastically.

Jackson carefully maneuvered the jeep through the closely packed rows, several times narrowly missing getting stuck in the slick red-brown soil that balled up beneath the wheels. Mud threatened to clog the wheel wells of the jeep. The rain had thoroughly soaked the soil making it so heavy the mud fell away from the undercarriage in huge clumps.

We drove for about a mile through the grove before Jackson killed the engine and we sat, thoroughly soaked and chilled, in the downpour.

"What now?" I asked.

"I don't know," he said. "I'm making this up as I go along. What about you?"

"The same," I said. "I won't know until I get there. Do you think there are any Vietcong out there?"

"Probably," he said. he reached behind his seat and removed a combat harness and AR-15. I heard the metal snick of the bolt as he chambered a round.

"We are a couple of idiots," I said. "I don't even have a pistol."

"Lucky for me," he said.

"Funny. Very funny."

"Let's go."

"Which way?"

"I'd guess that way. " He pointed to the front of the jeep. "The trees were planted in aisles, and a good bet is the workers moved together in line away from the house."

"Why do you say that?"

"That's the way the Master always planted the cotton."

"Lead on, Uncle Remus," I said and climbed from the jeep. "And try to get us there."

"That's no problem," he said and moved forward away from the jeep. "The problem's always in getting back."

Two hours later, we were flat on our stomachs under a bush. In front of us, a long, low bungalow stood at the end of five barrack huts. The barrack huts were dark, but light blazed from each window of the bungalow, and we could see the guards as they moved in pairs around the building. They were North Vietnamese.

"Well," I whispered. "Any ideas?"

"Yeah. Let's forget about it and go home."

"How many do you think?"

"Too many," he answered. "And that's funny. Why so many guards here?"

"What do you mean?"

"Why not guards in the trees? By the huts? The storehouse? Why just around the bungalow?

"Somebody important is in there. Somebody important enough to warrant guards from up north and not your VC farmer."

"Something else, too," I said. "What are they doing here?"

"Come on," he said and began wiggling his way backward.

I followed him back to the tree line, then we began a long traverse in a half-crouch, half-crawl, behind the huts to the back of the bungalow.

Suddenly, headlights flashed over the building, and the guards moved into position to face an approaching vehicle. Jackson tapped me on the shoulder and ran to the wall of the bungalow. I followed and pressed myself down against the earth next to the wall. Cautiously, we crawled to an open window and peered inside.

The room was sparingly furnished with a writing table and chair, a small, badly mended divan, two easy chairs, and an old gramophone in the corner. Two Vietnamese in business suits sat in the armchairs. They were drinking tea.

Jackson tugged at my arm, and I dropped flat to the ground as a pair of guards strolled past twenty feet away. I waited dry-mouthed for discovery, but they were watching the trees and not the house. They turned the corner, and I rose and carefully eased back to the window.

The two Vietnamese rose to their feet as the door opened, and Lautrec and Dupree walked into the room and closed the door behind them. The one nearest the window went to them and shook hands.

"Welcome, Inspector Dupree," he said in French. He nodded at Lautrec. "I trust you have good news for us?"

"Yes," Dupree said stiffly. His mouth was a thin line of distaste. "Delivery will be made tonight. He should be here within the hour. Might I suggest, Colonel Tin, that you move your men into the huts? He is an American,

202

you know, and he may have a certain reticence about dealing with the enemy."

The figure turned and made a small motion with his hand. The other Vietnamese left silently. I breathed a silent sigh of relief, then the name Dupree had used registered. Colonel Tin. Colonel Bei Tin? The legendary leader of Vietminh forces during the French war? Who else? I realized I was looking at one of the most wanted men in South Vietnam.

"You have done well," he was saying. "But I believe you had some trouble the other night?"

"Some," Dupree said. "But that should be resolved soon."

He turned as the door opened, and the Vietnamese returned.

"It is done," he said. "The guards are in each hut on either side of the road."

"Very good, Ngo Van Bang. Would you bring the, ah, package from the other room?" Bang nodded and glided from the room.

"I don't know why you keep him with you," Lautrec said. "He makes me nervous."

"Yes?" Colonel Tin smiled. "But that is precisely why I keep him with me. He makes everyone nervous. And he is very good, as you saw with that American reporter. Speaking of which," he turned to Dupree, "I believe we have again some trouble with yet another reporter? That does not speak well for you, Inspector Dupree. What have you done about him?"

Dupree shrugged. "It does not matter. Soon, the problem will be resolved."

"But when? How? Our situation is, ah, rather delicate. If you should be captured . . . well, you understand?"

He pointed to the table as Bang entered the room. Bang laid the package on the table, then moved to stand facing Dupree on his right. Lautrec moved to face him.

"I fully well understand persuasive interrogation,

Colonel Tin. I also know how useless it is to insist upon it. One is much better off to simply give them what they want. They will get it anyway. It's only a matter of time."

"Yes. I remember you were quite adept at it in the cellars of the *Sûreté d'Annam*. Too bad your prisoners did not share your opinion. But then they thought they were fighting for their country by keeping their silence."

"That was another time, another world," Dupree said. "We all make mistakes."

"Yes," Colonel Tin said and moved languidly back to sit in his chair. He lifted his cup, sipped from it, made a face, and set it down.

"I do detest cold tea. No, Bang," he said as the other made a move to refill his cup. "I have had enough. Would you care for some, Inspector Dupree? Lautrec? No?"

"We have since learned the errors of our ways," Dupree said, but his voice carried a hard edge to it that made his words seem a lie.

"Officially, you mean," Colonel Tin said mockingly. "But what about you, Inspector Dupree? Do you see the error of your ways? Do you agree with the policy of your country?"

"I am a Frenchman," he said stiffly.

"Ah, yes. But I wonder what *all* Frenchmen would say if they knew policies were being made by a few? Namely a few *colons* who are looking forward to reestablishing trade with the new Vietnam? More important, what would the Americans say?"

"This was our country before it was the Americans'," Dupree said.

"Correction," Colonel Tin said. "It was our country. It always was our country. And we have no intention of letting it become another colony for anyone." He laughed. "But really, it is quite humorous, is it not? Two countries both wanting exclusive trade rights with my tiny country. What could you both possibly want? Our rubber? No, it costs more to process our rubber than to make synthetic. Our gold? Tin? Copper? No, the expense of the war could never be regained by what little wealth could be taken from our mines. Now, what could we have that you each want so badly?"

"You know damn well what the United States wants," Dupree said. "The deep water port at Cam Ranh Bay. And they have it, thanks to the ninety-nine year lease granted them by the Saigon government. That will give them another port for shipping and maintaining a fleet in readiness against China. Very advantageous."

"Ah, yes. Save Vietnam from the communists. The domino theory the Americans are so fond of quoting. But what about the French? Why this sudden change of political heart? What do the French want so badly?"

"Trade," Dupree said. But I could tell from his voice he was unhappy about the way the conversation was going.

"Inspector Dupree," Colonel Tin said. He shook his head in feigned sadness. "Do you take us for fools? Do you think that we are not aware of Dr. Leroux's paper on the Annamite Fault? Let me see, what did he suggest might be found there?"

"Molybdenite," Dupree said. His eyes glittered malevolently at the Vietnamese. The word jolted me. Molly wasn't even a person. Molybdenite. Muhl had been on the story of the century. I remembered the books on his shelf and my feeling that he was trying to learn the country by osmosis. He was gathering information.

"Ah, yes. Molybdenite. Found in granite pegmatites and in veins with tin and copper materials. A very useful ore. Molybdenum is made from it. And correct me if I'm wrong, but is not molybdenum used in certain components necessary for guided missiles?"

Dupree remained silent. Colonel Tin laughed.

"Yes, I can see I am right. Tell me, what country owns about ninety percent of the world's molybdenite? The United States? Rather a monopoly, is it not? And what would happen to the military power of the world if the United States suddenly placed a restriction on the exporting of molybdenite? Hmm. Quite a subject for speculation, isn't it? Do you think the United States knows of Dr. Leroux's paper?"

"No," Dupree said.

"But it would have if that reporter had not been silenced. And now we have another reporter. I repeat: what have you done about him? Is that our friend?"

Dimly, I became aware of the heavy growl of a truck as it ground its way up the road to the bungalow, but I paid it no mind. At last, I knew why Muhl had been killed. It was not for the pilfering of PX supplies, nor the heroin market, but something far larger. Something that would have earned him his own Pulitzer, the foreign desk, and eventually the publisher's chair at the *Times*. Once about every fifty years such a story comes along, and he had fallen into it.

"Yes," Dupree said, after checking through the door. "May I introduce Captain Abraham Lenwald of the United States Army, Sergeant Larry Bowman, and the answer to what you call 'my problem'?"

Captain Lenwald walked into the room and stepped to where he could see both Bang and Lautrec. Then Bowman appeared, dragging Rachel with him.

31

STUNNED, I DROPPED below the windowsill and grabbed Jackson by the arm.

"Rachel," I whispered urgently to him. He pressed his fingers to my lips and shook his head fiercely at me. I nodded and swallowed heavily. For some inexplicable reason, my throat burned.

"What is this?" Colonel Tin's voice drifted through the open window. I did not raise my head; there was no need to. Each detail of the room was indelibly printed upon my mind.

"She is the mistress of the reporter," Dupree explained smoothly. "He is very attached to her."

"I see," Colonel Tin said. His words were doubtful and a touch sarcastic. "But do you believe a man such as Mr. Edwards will allow his personal feelings to interfere with his work?"

"In this matter, yes," Dupree continued. "He is not a strong man. She means much to him since he is older than she. Much older. He has become very foolish with his attachment to her. It is the weakness of old men when a beautiful young woman seems to find them attractive at a crucial point in their lives when they first realize their own mortality and despair of ever loving again. Such men once again feel young, and they are most reluctant to let go of that feeling, and so they do very foolish things."

"Perhaps," Colonel Tin said. "But surely this man will realize that she is lost to him. She knows all now, since you have brought her here. We cannot let her go back to him whatever he promises."

"That does not matter," Dupree said. "He will continue to hope otherwise."

"Why don't you simply kill him?" Captain Lenwald said. He spoke very bad French in a flat and emotionless voice. "It will be certain if you kill him."

Cautiously, I raised my head to the windowsill and peeked in. Rachel stood between Colonel Tin and Dupree. I could see the fear in the slight trembling of her legs, but she stared defiantly at Colonel Tin, contempt and disgust in her eyes, her jaw set.

"That would be too much of a coincidence," Dupree argued, as Colonel Tin looked thoughtful. "Two reporters from the same newspaper in less than six months? I would not believe such a thing myself."

"And what is it you wish me to do?" Colonel Tin asked. He moved forward and fingered her touseled hair. His thin face creased into a smile, but the smile did not touch his eyes as he studied the tilt of her breasts, the swell of her hips. The air seemed suddenly charged with animal want. Rachel slapped his hand away.

"Keep your goddamn hands to yourself, you slimy son of a bitch," she said. The skin tightened over her high cheekbones. I was alternately proud of her and fearful of Tin's plans for her.

"Take her with you when you return to your home tomorrow," Dupree said. "That will give us the leverage we need with Con Edwards."

"An excellent idea," Tin said. His hand reached out for her hair again. Rachel let his fingers entwine themselves in her curls, then suddenly lifted a knee into his groin. He doubled over in pain, his hands cupping himself against the agony shooting through his stomach. Rachel spun and raced for the window, then froze as Bowman's voice cut through the room.

208

"Don't!" he yelled. The single word was punctuated by the sound of a hammer being thumbed back to full cock.

She paused and turned slowly to face him. He held a .45 leveled at her chest.

"Don't," he said again softly. "If I miss, they won't." He nodded at Lautrec and Bang. Both had drawn small automatics from their pockets.

Rachel's shoulders slumped, and she waited as Tin slowly and painfully straightened. He stepped in front of her and slapped her brutally across the face.

"Perhaps I was mistaken," he said. A thin strand of saliva trickled from the corner of his mouth. "My soldiers will be grateful for my gift to them."

"Your soldiers?" Captain Lenwald said. His eyes narrowed as he looked suspiciously from Bang to Tin. "What soldiers?"

"It is nothing," Dupree said quickly, soothingly. "Simply a name for the men of the Binh Xuyen."

"Uh-huh," Lenwald said. His eyes flicked to Tin and back to Dupree. "What do you think, Bowman?"

"I don't know, boss," the lanky Tennessean said. "Sounds like a nigger in the pantry to me." The muzzle of his .45 now pointed at Dupree. "Why don't you tell them to put those peashooters away until we sort this out?"

"What is the problem?" Tin asked.

"We don't do business with the enemy," Lenwald said.

"You mean the northerners?" Tin laughed. "Be reasonable. What do you carry that would be of interest to the National Liberation Front? Cigarettes? Nylons? Perhaps whisky? We deal in commodities, my friend, not arms or munitions."

Lenwald studied him closely for a long minute, considering, then nodded.

"All right," he said. "We'll deal with you. Where's the package?"

"On the table," Dupree said and stepped aside.

Lenwald crossed to the table, carefully keeping himself from crossing between Lautrec and Bang and Bowman. He took a knife from his pocket and burrowed a small hole in the corner of the package and tasted the white powder.

"You have a deal," he said, turning to Dupree. He looked at Colonel Tin. "But we will not come here again. It is too dangerous. Delivery must be made from now on in Saigon."

"Let us say in Dakow," Tin said. "The police in Saigon are becoming more difficult to work with."

"The old Vieux Moulin?" Dupree suggested. "You may pick up your payment there. We will bring a truck to your warehouse and load from there."

"How?" Bowman asked. " 'Scuse me, boss, but that don't seem possible. How are they going to look like Americans?"

"Americans will take delivery," Tin said, smiling thinly at Bowman's skepticism. "Like all soldiers who fight in a war, there are some who find it profitable to, uh, shall we say 'terminate' their obligations earlier than expected?"

"Deserters," Lenwald said. His mouth twisted in contempt. "How can one trust such men?"

"One can't," Tin said. "But there is little opportunity for work in their situation, and they are expendable."

"There is that," Lenwald said. "Very well. The twenty-fifth of each month send two trucks to the warehouse. One driver will be from Nha Trang, the other from Da Nang. That will be five days from payday, and we will be very busy as the unit PXs will be restocking in anticipation of sales on the thirtieth. On that day, one of us will meet you at the Capriccio. Have the package in an old briefcase of the type with straps. We will exchange the briefcase thusly over a drink."

Tin smiled at Lenwald's rejection of the old Vieux Moulin for the exchange.

"You are a careful man," he said.

"The careless are dead."

"It will be as you say," Tin agreed. "One package per truck, the thirtieth."

Lenwald shook his head. "No. Three for the two trucks. Three kilos. The risk, as you say, is becoming greater."

Tin hesitated, then nodded.

"Very well. But do not become too greedy, my friend."

"What about the woman?"

"She will go with me," Tin said. "Do not concern yourself with her."

"I don't," Lenwald said. He slipped behind Bowman and left. There was a slight pause, then the engine of the truck turned over and caught. Bowman nodded to Dupree and backed from the room. He kept his eyes on Lautrec and Bang until the door closed in front of him. Moments later, we could hear the truck being shifted through its gears as it moved down the road.

"The fool," Tin said explosively. "His merchandise means little to me. I would have given him five kilos for each delivery. It is more important to us for the Americans to have the heroin than for us to have their luxuries."

"When do you go back north?" Dupree asked.

"Tonight," Tin said. "I understand the Americans will enter the Iron Triangle at Ben Cat tomorrow. I wish to be gone by then. That is only a few kilometers from here."

"Lautrec and I will go to Bien Hoa tonight and return to Saigon tomorrow," Dupree said. He looked at Rachel and gave her an apologetic smile.

"I am most sorry, my dear, but you will be unable to accompany me."

"You are a pimp, Dupree," she said contemptuously. "You'd sell anything."

"Yes," he said. "For my country, yes."

"Your country is a whore, and you its pimp. This won't stop Con, you know."

"For your sake, you better hope it does," he said darkly. He nodded at Lautrec and left. Lautrec followed him through the door and closed it gently behind him.

"Tell the others we shall leave in an hour," Tin said curtly to Bang. "One hour. We must be gone by then." He faced Rachel as the Vietnamese walked silently from the room.

"And now, my dear, we have one hour."

Rachel made a move towards the door, but was brought up shortly by a pistol Tin removed from beneath his coat.

"I think not," he said softly. "I fully intend for that hour to be very meaningful for both of us. In there."

He gestured towards a beaded curtain that covered a doorway to his right. Rachel hesitated, then her shoulders sagged in resignation, and she walked with slow steps through the curtain and disappeared.

32

I DROPPED TO my knees beside Jackson and shook his shoulder.

"We have to do something," I said frantically.

He shook off my arm and kept his attention on the darkness away from the house.

"What?" he asked softly. "What can we do? We have only this." He lifted the AR-15. "And the .45. They've got ten times that. We start anything, and we're dead."

"What chance does she have?" I demanded. "You know what he's got planned for her."

"We're in over our heads. You should have listened to Lautrec when he warned you."

"Would you have listened to him?"

"No," he said. "I would have killed him and been done with it."

"Then you would never have known the truth," I said.

"And you think you know it now? You're a jerk."

"Please. I love her."

"Shit," he said. I could hear his sigh of resignation. "Come on."

He looked quickly through the window, then stood and slipped through the opening. I followed, trying to keep my clothing from rasping over the sill. He didn't hesitate, but moved soundlessly over the rush mats to the left of the beaded curtain and flattened himself against the wall. I slipped to the wall opposite him, my mouth dry, my legs shaking. He took two deep breaths, then gently, quietly, eased the beaded strands aside and slipped through the doorway. I edged around the opposite corner and found myself in the bedroom. I had a brief flash of a cracked wardrobe, a straight chair, and a narrow bed. Rachel lay on the dirty mattress, eyes closed tightly, while Tin rose slowly from the footboard where he knelt to strap her legs to the iron rungs with leather thongs. He had used the room for this before: the thongs were well-oiled, but the knots were furred and the ends wrapped back against the leather with black electrical tape.

He smiled as we entered and said, "You are very foolish. What can you hope to gain but your deaths?"

He made a small move towards his jacket draped over the back of the chair, but Jackson stepped forward and jammed the barrel of the AR-15 hard against his mouth. His lips split, and his front teeth disappeared. He grunted in surprise and tried to reel back from the savage attack, but Jackson moved with him and slammed his head against the wall.

"Ours or yours, pretty boy," he said softly, using the coarse French word for homosexual. "Makes no difference to me. I already know I'm dead. How is she?"

The last was spoken to me. I hastily moved to the side of the bed as Rachel's eyes opened in wide surprise.

"Con," she exclaimed. "How . . ."

"Later," I said. I fumbled at the knots securing her hands to the headboard.

"Cut 'hem," Jackson said and tossed his knife on the bed. He kept his eyes on Tin. "But cut them long. We'll need them."

I cut the knots and helped Rachel to her feet. She rubbed her wrists and glared at Tin.

"Kill him," she said tonelessly.

"Rachel," I began.

"Shut up. It wasn't you tied to the bed." She moved to Jackson's side. "Kill him. Now. Here. While I'm watching so I can see him die."'

"No," Jackson said. "We need him. Where's his pistol?"

"In his jacket. He put it in his jacket after he tied my hands."

"Get it."

Reluctantly, I reached for the jacket, but Rachel snatched it from my hands and pulled the pistol from an inside pocket. She glanced at me briefly, her eyes filled with contempt. I hesitated, puzzled by what I had seen, and she turned back to Jackson.

"Got it," she said.

"Good. Place the muzzle against his temple. If he moves, kill him. She will, you know," he added to Tin. "She doesn't need much reason."

Tin didn't answer him. I doubt if he could have: his mouth was a brutal wound, but I could feel no pity for him. His eyes, however, glittered venomously like an adder at Jackson.

Rachel jammed the pistol against Tin's temple. Tin ignored her and kept his eyes on Jackson as the burly sergeant gathered the leather thongs from the bed and approached him.

"Lie down," he ordered. Carefully, Tin dropped to his knees and stretched out full-length on the floor. Rachel followed him down, the pistol pressed firmly to his temple. Jackson roughly twisted Tin's hands behind his back and lashed them firmly together. Then he ripped a piece of cloth from his shirt, rolled it into a ball, and gagged him.

"You take them back to the jeep," he said to me upon rising. "I'll follow. If anything happens, don't stop. Get to the jeep, and take him to the authorities. Understand?"

"Yes. What about you?"

"What about me? Don't be stupid. If I'm not there, then I'll never be there." He looked at Tin. "One more thing. If he gives you any trouble, kill him. Don't try anything fancy or noble. Just put a bullet in his brains, and get out as fast as you can. Let's go."

Rachel slipped through the window and kept the pistol steady on Tin as he clambered awkwardly through the window with his hands tied behind his back. He fell to the ground and tried to get up, but she never moved to help him. I landed beside him and pulled him to his feet. He glared at her.

"You first," Jackson whispered to me. "Then Tin and Rachel. Go as straight as you can. You stay close to Tin," he said to Rachel. "Move out."

I began to walk rapidly into the stand of rubber trees. The rain had slackened, but there was no moon, and every shadow was an ominous threat. Mice rustled across our path, and I could feel larger animals moving off to the side and watching our progress. I could taste the fear in my mouth, coppery like new pennies, and I moved faster. Behind me, Tin stumbled against clods of earth as he fought to keep his balance. He had told Bang that they were to leave in an hour. Roughly half of that time had passed, and we still had at least a quarter-mile to go when I heard the outbreak behind me as Bang discovered Tin was missing. I wanted to run, but I knew those behind me wouldn't be able to keep up without killing Tin. I forced myself to maintain the same pace and tried to ignore the ominous shadows.

A sudden burst of gunfire behind us made me jump, and my bowels threatened to loosen. I glanced back. Tin was still on my heels, and Rachel behind him. She angrily motioned me forward with her free hand and jammed the pistol in Tin's back. I looked for Jackson, but couldn't see him.

"Move, goddamn you!" Rachel said urgently.

I grabbed Tin's arm to steady him and began to trot. My lungs gasped for air, and my side burned like a brand

216

by the time we reached the jeep. I pushed Tin into the passenger seat. Rachel climbed in behind him. She grabbed his hair and yanked his head back until he was staring up at the starless sky.

"We don't want him jumping, do we?" she said. "Drive!"

"Jackson . . ." I said.

"Remember what he said. He's counting on us to do just that. Now, drive!"

A burst of gunfire, closer than the last, decided me. I leapt into the seat and ground the starter. The engine caught, then roared. I slammed the gears into first, spun the wheel in a tight circle, and drove out of the trees back onto the road. I kept the blackout lights on until we rounded the first curve, then boosted to brights, dropped the jeep into fourth gear, and firmly placed the accelerator to the floorboards and pointed the nose of the jeep towards Highway One and Saigon. The gunfire behind dimmed to a faint crackle, then stopped.

33

IT WAS LATE afternoon by the time Rachel and I could leave Colonel Black's office and go to the apartment. The questions seemed endless and highly repetitive, first with Black and then with Le Duc Trinh, to whom Black had delivered Tin. From the glitter in Trinh's eyes, I knew Tin would be lucky if he ever saw Poulo Condore. Black had dispatched a special team to the Michelin Plantation to pick up Jackson. They had found him, badly wounded, but still alive at the west end of the plantation. He had led Tin's men away from us and eluded them by crawling into a septic tank after being wounded. He had been taken to the 93rd Evac Hospital, where he was awaiting transportation back to the States. Dupree had been arrested on the terrace of the Continental. Although a massive search was conducted throughout the city, Lautrec had disappeared. Captain Lenwald and Sergeant Bowman were arrested at the warehouse and the heroin confiscated.

I sent my story (cleared by Black's censors) to the *Times* from Black's office while Rachel was being questioned.

"You were very lucky," Black had said, when we were finally together in his office.

"Somebody had to do it," I replied. My eyes were gritty from lack of sleep, and I could smell the sour odor of dried perspiration in my clothes. Rachel had dark circles under her eyes, and hard lines of exhaustion were deeply etched into the corners of her eyes and mouth.

218

"That's what we thought," Black said. "But we never expected you to go the last lap alone."

"What?" I struggled to clear the fog from my mind. "I don't understand. *You* were aware of everything?"

"Yes," he said. "We suspected Dupree from the beginning and had an inkling of Lenwald and Bowman's involvement with him, but we had no proof. If we had mounted an investigation, news would have leaked out. It would have created a scandal when we could least afford it if our suspicions were proven wrong. We needed help from the outside. The question was, who?"

"So you chose me to do your dirty work," I said bitterly.

"No," he said softly. "We chose Muhl."

"What?" I straightened in my chair. "Muhl?"

"Yes. We did not think you were the type we needed. We needed someone willing to take risks, someone eager to work, not only on a story, but someone who was willing to become involved. You have never involved yourself in anything. We needed a participant, not a spectator."

"You killed him," I said hotly.

"Did I? Or did you, Mr. Edwards? It was not I who limited Muhl in his work. It was not I who refused him the stories he needed to advance himself. It was not I who took his place on the junket to Nha Trang. But," he continued, "I must accept partial blame. I did arrange for him to be given the information he needed to begin his investigation. We all had a hand in his execution, Mr. Edwards. Not just one man."

We made a small detour to Cholon on our way back to the apartment. Although we were both dead tired, I felt obligated to tell Phuong the end of the story that had caused her so much misery and pain.

Ha Bo cautiously opened the door to our knock and stepped aside as he recognized me. He gave Rachel a cursory glance as she trailed me in, then dismissed her: women never interested him, other than his sister.

I looked at his childish expression, eager and happy to see someone he thought of as a friend, and tried to suppress an involuntary shudder as I remembered the screams of terror from Dupree's men when he suddenly dropped into their midst in the warehouse.

"How is Minh?" I asked quickly. I caught Rachel's look of surprise out of the corner of my eye and remembered I had forgotten to tell her Phuong's real name.

"She much better," he said, his face beaming. "But she worry."

"About what?" I asked, as I moved into the room and willed myself not to slump into the chair behind the table.

"Jack-san," he said. He frowned as he tried to concentrate. I waited.

"Where Jack-san?" he finally asked, unable to put into words the feelings that worked at his subconscious.

"Hospital," I said, slipping into the monosyllabic patois easiest for him to understand. "He hurt very bad."

A terrible shade came across his features. He clenched his massive hands, and I watched in awe as the muscles rippled beneath his shirt. I was glad I wasn't one of the "bad mans." Or, I reflected, was I?

"Same bad mans hurt Minh?"

"Yes," I said and quickly added as his face settled into cold fury, "But they gone now. Police take them."

He gestured violently. "Con not know police same bad mans?"

"Police different," I answered and immediately remembered Trinh and Loan and Loan's public execution of the Vietcong suspect. Was there really any difference between Trinh and Loan and Dupree and Lautrec? I looked at Rachel: she stared at me impassively. Contorted images of her and Black and Muhl began to flicker against the screen of my memory. I tried to force them away.

"Police same police," Ha Bo insisted. Then his voice edge with concern. "Jack-san no come back?"

I shrugged. "I don't know."

His face worked as he tried to give voice to his thoughts. Finally, he gave up and said urgently, "Con see Minh now. Yes?"

"Yes," I said. "Yes, I see Minh now."

We walked into the room where Phuong lay. Her eyes followed us as we crossed the tiny distance to her bed. With Ha Bo in the room, it seemed smaller than it had before. Her eyebrows were raised in query.

"Hi, Phuong," I said softly. I reached for her hand and pressed it gently. "How are you feeling?"

She waved my question away and motioned for something with which to write. I handed her a notebook and pen.

"It's over," I said, as she began to trace block letters on the paper. "The police have arrested everyone except Lautrec. He got away. But I don't think we will have to worry about him."

She turned the pad so I could read what she had written: JACKSON.

"I'm sorry," I said. "He was badly hurt. They are sending him home."

A small tear trickled down her pockmarked cheek. She raised a hand to wipe it away.

"I'm sorry," I said awkwardly. "I didn't know."

She scribbled rapidly on the pad and turned it to me.
HOW JACKSON HURT?

"He stayed behind so we could get away," I said. "We had a prisoner. A big man from the north."

YOU LEAVE HIM?

"He wanted it that way," I tried to explain. "He told us what to do."

LAUTREC AWAY NOT DEAD.

"Don't worry about him," I said soothingly. "The police will find him. He won't be causing any trouble."

221

She gave me a contemptuous look and scribbled furiously. I read as she wrote.

YOU FOOL.

"I'm sorry. We did what we thought was best," I said lamely, but I could feel the words falling flat as they left my mouth.

Her eyes went opaque, and she handed the pad and pen back to me. She turned her head away from me. Her shoulders shook as she started to cry. I started to reach for her, but Ha Bo's huge hand stopped me. I turned to look at him.

"You go now," he said. His face was granite. "We no want you now. I take care Minh. No need you."

I looked at Rachel and saw the same contempt I had seen at the plantation when I had tried to get the pistol from Tin's jacket pocket.

"Go now," Ha Bo said insistently.

I didn't argue and followed Rachel from the room and down the stairs. The door clicked shut behind me. The sound seemed final in the narrow hallway. I tried to convince myself that Phuong was being unfair. Everything was done to find the truth. But, for some strange reason, that seemed false to me now. What was the truth? Had I found it, or had I found a partial truth revealed only by different lies from the ones I had encountered at the start of my search?

I remembered Black's final words as I opened the door to the apartment: many hands did execute Muhl. I stepped aside for Rachel to enter. She moved tiredly to the easy chair next to the French doors and sank thankfully into its depths.

"Drink?" I asked and walked to the liquor table.

"Please. Scotch. No ice. No soda."

I poured two glasses with generous measures and crossed to the chair. She murmured her thanks and took it gratefully. I sat on the sofa across from her, rested my feet on the rattan coffee table, and studied her. She had

222

been strangely silent on our way back from Cholon. I remembered Dupree's words: had I done so many foolish things that he had spoken of? And, most important, had I done them for the reason Dupree had suggested?

"Tell me, Rachel," I said, after she had swallowed half her drink. "Who was the intermediary between Colonel Black and Muhl?"

She opened her eyes and stared at me. Her eyes were large in the soft light: I could see the white around the pale blue irises and deep within them, a look of sorrow. Then it disappeared as she raised her glass and sipped carefully from it.

"Why?" I asked.

"It was my job," she said. "We needed someone not connected with the military. Muhl was ambitious, looking for that big story that would make his career."

"When?" I swallowed heavily, my throat suddenly dry with foreboding.

"When you went to Hue," she said. Her eyes held mine hypnotically. I didn't want to hear the rest, but knew I had to.

"Why him? Why not me? Wouldn't it have been easier to try to recruit me?"

"No," she said firmly. "The assignment called for total involvement and for someone without scruples, someone who was willing to take a chance. You have always played it safe, using people as a buffer between yourself and the world. You remain too detached, too emotionless."

"That's not true," I protested weakly.

"Isn't it?" She smiled, but there was no warmth in the smile. "Then why didn't you push ahead with your story on Major Powell?"

"I did it for us," I said. I could hear the desperation in my voice, but I didn't care.

"Did you? Or was that another way of keeping the

world at bay? What was more important, Con, us or the truth?" She shook her head. "You claim to search for the truth, but when you find it, you back away if it affects you. You only got involved after Muhl's death made it a news story that kept your personal life out of the picture. That's all your life has been Con: just stories."

Tears burned my eyes, and I lifted my glass, drank, then crossed to the liquor table and poured the glass to the brim. But I knew even as I raised the glass to my lips that no amount of Scotch would fill the hollowness inside me at that moment.

"Hong Kong would be lovely this time of year," she said quietly. "I still have some leave coming. Should I take it?"

I took a deep drink and swallowed heavily as the Scotch burned down my throat and dislodged the lump there.

"Con?"

I breathed deeply. The image of an empty apartment flashed through my mind. I wasn't ready for that. Not yet. But I knew that prolonging the final break would only make it worse. The good times were over, and trying to stay together and rebuild what we once had would only result in bitterness. I crossed to the French doors and eased them open: the tamarind trees were a startling green against the golden sunlight and the streets empty as people waited out the noon heat.

"Con?"

"Yes," I said, staring at the emptiness. I swallowed the remainder of the Scotch in my glass and held the empty glass tight against my chest as I forced down the gag reflex. "Yes, why don't you do that?"

If you have enjoyed this book and would like to receive details of other Walker Adventure titles, please write to:

Adventure Editor
Walker and Company
720 Fifth Avenue
New York, NY 10019